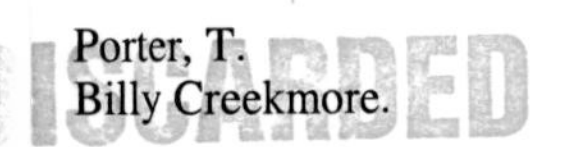

Billy Creekmore

Billy Creekmore

by Tracey Porter

JOANNA COTLER BOOKS
An Imprint of HarperCollins*Publishers*

ACKNOWLEDGMENTS

My father, Bruce Porter, and my stepfather, Larry Short, played important roles in the early stages of this book. I would like to thank my dad and my brother, James Porter, for being my traveling companions and fellow researchers during our road trip through Appalachia, and my stepdad and his wife, Roberta Short, for taking me to the wonderful Ringling Museum of the Circus in Sarasota. I am very grateful to the librarians, archivists, and scholars at that museum's library, and to those at the West Virginia Historical Museum. Special thanks go to Professor Ken Heckler of Charleston, Ringling archivist Dawn Shongood, and Leroy White, my tour guide at the Beckley Exhibition Coal Mine.

My deep gratitude for their support, careful reading, and great insight goes to Justin Chanda, Karen Nagel, and Joanna Cotler. No writer could have more talented editors or a more gracious publisher, and I feel very fortunate to work with them.

I want to thank my mother, Susan Morcone, for her constant support and encouragement, and my children, Sarah and Sam, for putting up with a mother who gave up cooking so she could finish a book.

Finally, I want to thank my husband, Sandy Corner, for his love and companionship, and for always encouraging me to tell my stories.

Billy Creekmore

 For information address HarperCollins Children's Books, a division of HarperCollins Publishers, 1350 Avenue of the Americas, New York, NY 10019. www.harpercollinschildrens.com

Library of Congress Cataloging-in-Publication Data

Porter, Tracey.

Billy Creekmore / by Tracey Porter. — 1st ed.

p. cm.

Summary: In 1905, ten-year-old Billy is taken from an orphanage to live with an aunt and uncle he never knew he had, and he enjoys his first taste of family life until his work in a coal mine and involvement with a union brings trouble, then he joins a circus in hopes of finding his father.

ISBN-13: 978-0-06-077570-4 (trade bdg.) — ISBN-13: 978-0-06-077571-1 (lib. bdg.)

[1. Self-reliance—Fiction. 2. Orphanages—Fiction. 3. Coal mines and mining—Fiction. 4. Circus—Fiction. 5. West Virginia—History—To 1950—Fiction.] I. Title.

PZ7.P83395Bil 2007 2007000001

[Fic]—dc22 CIP

AC

Typography by Neil Swaab

1 2 3 4 5 6 7 8 9 10

First Edition

For my son, Sam

Part One

CHAPTER ONE

THE STRANGE CIRCUMSTANCES *of My Birth* *and* *How I Came to Be Raised at* THE GUARDIAN ANGELS HOME FOR BOYS

Folks say I'm bound to be unlucky in life, for I was born at midnight on a Friday, the thirteenth of December, and Peggy says it's certain I can commune with spirits. But I ain't never seen any ghosts, not even my own mother, and wouldn't that be the ghost I'd see if I could?

Peggy put down her knife to give it some thought. "Maybe she figures you won't recognize her. After all, you were only hours old when she died."

"Or maybe she's a fearful ghost who won't come to me since I'm what killed her. Now, don't shake your head, Peggy! I know what folks say! I heard Mrs. Beadle tell you."

"I don't believe it, Billy, and I don't want you to, either."

But I did.

The midwife who delivered me is kin to Mrs. Beadle, so the story was common knowledge. My birth alone nearly killed my mother, but it was the shock of me that did her in. It was 1895, the coldest winter in West Virginia's recorded history. I entered the world as the clock struck twelve, silent and limp, my eyes closed. Then, as the midwife slapped some life into me, I started speaking. And it warn't gurgles or babbles either, but real words. I raised a finger and pointed into space saying, "There! There!" my eyes shut, like I was stuck between worlds. It was unsettling and eerie, such a frightening thing to see that it stopped my mother's heart. My pa, wild with loss, fearful and distressed, ran out in the night and never returned.

"What about your pa?" asked Peggy. "Do you ever see the ghost of your pa?"

"My pa's not dead. At least he warn't at Christmas. He sent me a picture postcard."

"Well, where is he then?"

"I don't know. He travels about and sends me a postcard every now and then."

"How sad, Billy!" Her face puckered up, and her eyes got wet. "Oh, but it's not right to abandon your child, no matter how brokenhearted you might be!" She turned back to her chopping. Pieces of carrot flew about, and she moved quick and graceful in the kitchen despite her great size. I had risen before dawn to drink some tea and have a little talk. We were buddies, Peggy and me.

"Tell me, Billy. What was on the postcard then?"

"Picture of a paddleboat on the Ohio River. But that ain't no clue to where he's at. I get picture postcards from him once a year or more, all showin' sight-seein' type things—a suspension bridge, train station, a statue in a park. . . ."

"Does he leave an address for you to write him back?" asked Peggy.

"Nope. But he always writes the same thing—'with love from your pa.'"

"Oh!" said Peggy in a voice sharp with pain, just like she got pricked with a pin. She pulled me into her arms to rock me back and forth like a baby. I quick set down my tea so I didn't scald us. "Imagine leaving your only son in an orphanage while you rove about seeing the glories and curiosities of the world!"

One of the buttons down the back of her blouse popped off, and it was hard to breathe, being squeezed so tight in her doughy arms. Otherwise, I'm sure I'd have cried with her at my pitiful state. I was ten years old, and I'd be lying if I said I didn't want to be held and loved every now and then. I was alone in the world, my mother dead, my father traveling about in places unknown, too filled with mourning and dread to raise me as his son.

In time Peggy let up on me, but before she did, she held me at arm's length and looked me plain in the face.

"Do you see spirits, Billy? Any at all? Do they talk to you?"

I shook my head. Truth be told, I was afraid of having the gift of communicating with spirits. It's what killed my mother and made my father leave. "Sometimes I sense 'em, though," I admitted to Peggy. "I'll feel my skin tingle right here," I said, touching my temples, "and it's almost like they're hoverin' off to the side, just where I can't see, but I ain't never seen one. Sometimes I pretend to see 'em when I don't. But please don't tell no one I said so."

"I won't," said Peggy in a worried voice, "but one day they'll come to you, and until then you better stop pretending. Telling lies about seeing spirits is an awful sin."

"I know," I said. "But I don't think God minds if I tell a story to give folks somethin' to think about, or else to save myself from Mr. Beadle. Remember how bad he hurt Herbert Mullens?"

"Heavens, yes, poor lamb," said Peggy. Then she crossed herself and moved her lips. Herbert was just a sparrow of a boy, slight and twitchy, only six years old when Mr. Beadle tore into him for dropping a basket of eggs. He was so scared, so injured by the beating, that he stopped talking and had to be taken to the home for children who are deaf and blind and otherwise can't find a way in the world. Peggy said a quick prayer for him, as was her habit whenever she heard of Mr. Beadle thrashing one of the boys. No doubt she'd be praying for him later on. After she cooked our breakfast, she walked all the way to Albright to go to mass, for she was Catholic, and couldn't go to our chapel.

"Whatever your reasons, Billy, don't get used to lying. You'll be lost if you do. Promise God in your prayers that you won't lie no more."

"I will, Peggy," I answered. I looked at her long as I could, but shifted my eyes to the ground as soon as she went back to her cooking. I couldn't bear to tell her that praying didn't make no sense to me, at least not the prayers the preacher and the Beadles made us say.

By now light was edging over the mountains. A pot of oatmeal was bubbling away, and four plates of biscuits, one for each table of boys, waited on the counter. It was Sabbath day, and, for one day of the week, Mr. Beadle wanted us well fed. Chapel was after breakfast, and he didn't want none of us fainting from hunger or disturbing the services with a growling stomach. I grabbed a biscuit and was all ready to pop it in my mouth when Peggy grabbed my wrist.

"Hide yourself, Billy," she whispered, for sure enough Mr. Beadle was swinging open the door and stomping into the dining hall. I slipped under a table while Peggy made herself busy rattling the pots and bustling about.

"Good morning, Peggy." Mr. Beadle's voice filled the room like a preacher's. From my hiding place I could see he was wearing his work boots, a dreadful sight, for it meant Mr. Beadle had some project in mind. He was plum full of himself, as usual. He went on and on in his proud voice, giving Peggy directions about using lard instead of butter and not spoiling us with sugar in our oatmeal. He counted the cans on the pantry shelf, eyed the salamis hanging from the ceiling, and emptied the purse Peggy kept behind the chopping block. He counted the coins, telling Peggy she was spending too much on our meals, then went on to describe the fancy plans he had for his and Mrs. Beadle's Sunday dinner.

"Our dear friend Mr. Colder will be dining with us this evening, and I'd like you to serve chicken, if you please. Chicken with dumplings."

"Yes, sir, Mr. Beadle. Just as you like it. I surely will, sir." Peggy had her own cleverness with words. She warn't fast with a story like I was, but she knew just what to say and what tone to use with Mr. Beadle. I saw her skirts sway, and I knew she was nodding respectful at his every word.

"A nice, plump chicken, Peggy. And a pie! A peach pie! Only the best for Mr. Colder, our dear friend, who is taking on another of our boys to apprentice in the glass factory."

"Is he now, Mr. Beadle? And isn't that a wonderful thing, learning such a valuable trade as that."

Mr. Colder was the foreman at the glass factory over in Morgantown, and he often came to Sunday dinner. Every now and then, he took one of the older boys away to work in the factory.

"Yes, indeed, Peggy. Wonderful it is for the fortunate lad, and for us, too, I might add. For as you well know, boys eat so much as they get older! The expense, Peggy! The expense of running an orphanage for these destitute boys of ignoble parentage! Why, Mrs. Beadle and I feed and clothe them, only to live like paupers ourselves!

And my dear wife is ruining her frail health trying to educate them! Surely our reward lies in Heaven, for our charity brings us no earthly riches."

I was of two minds at that moment. One was reacting in a downright negative way to his speech about himself, and the other was busy pondering who was lucky enough to be leaving the orphanage. How in Heaven's name could Mr. Beadle think of himself as a charitable man! Why, we boys were being charitable to *him*! We slaved away, working his farm, and getting nothing for it but beatings, rags, and barely enough food to keep us alive.

All of us looked forward to leaving the orphanage and going to work in the glass factory. Why, a boy could make sixty-five cents a day, and it was a glorious thing to get away from Mr. Beadle and see something new in the world. Would it be Walter Barnes or Willis Dawson? Both of them was twelve, but Walter was tall for his age and Willis didn't seem to have no sense. Once I overheard Mr. Colder tell the Beadles that only small boys could tend the furnace. How old was Meek Jones? I wondered. Warn't he old enough? He was smaller than the others, that's for sure. If I had money, I'd bet on Walter Barnes, I thought. He's big for his age, but nimble enough. I myself would be happy as pie to go off to work in Mr. Colder's factory. Waiting two more years was plain torture.

On and on Mr. Beadle went about all the hardships he and his wife suffered while providing for us boys. Peggy listened and murmured, "God loves you for it, sir," and "Rest assured your glory lies in Heaven," while stirring the pot. In general, I'm more curious than angry, so I was able to sit still and wonder instead of rushing out to tell Mr. Beadle how wrong he was about himself.

Soon the boys came stumbling in, bleary eyed and hungry. Peggy eyed me to get going. It was easy to scoot out and join the group unseen. Altogether, there was nineteen of us boys, and when Mr. Beadle was in the dining hall, we followed the rules for mealtime with a deadly seriousness. We took our places at the table, prayed piously, then began to eat.

"Lord help us," whispered little Rufus Twilly to the table of boys. "Mr. Beadle's in his work boots." Rufus slept in the cot next to me and warn't more than eight years old. He was freckled all over, even on his eyelids.

"Sure is," I replied. "I heard him tell Peggy Mr. Colder's comin' to supper tonight. Bet he's got his mind set on fixin' the fence that goes round his house. You know how he likes things to look just so when Mr. Colder comes to visit."

"Just as long as he's far away from me," answered Rufus.

"He'll fix that fence, but he won't fix our roof," said Walter Barnes. "Rain soaks us in our beds at night but he don't care none." Walter was slumping over his bowl of oatmeal with his knees knocking the underside of the table. I was about to mention I heard Mr. Colder would be taking one of the older boys away with him, but I thought better of it. Walter seemed to be turning meaner and meaner as time wore on. No telling how he might handle this type of news.

It was the grandest meal of the week, with two biscuits for everyone, but none of us could enjoy it. Mr. Beadle walked between the tables, carrying his hickory switch and watching us like we was convicts. It warn't no way to eat.

"Hurry, boys!" His voice boomed through the dining hall. Spoons clinked against bowls, and the plate of biscuits emptied lickety-split. "The preacher is waiting for you, and there are chores after that. There's no rest for those disposed to sin, not even on the Sabbath!"

"Ever notice how we're more wicked on the days he needs somethin' done?" asked Walter Barnes.

"Hush!" whispered Rufus. I shot Walter a glance, too. Just being around Walter made us nervous. Mr. Beadle was likely to turn around and give anyone near him a few lashes for encouraging him. Maybe Mr. Beadle would send Walter off to the glassworks, seeing how he was near big enough to stand up to him.

A few boys stayed behind to sweep the crumbs and help Peggy clean the dishes. But soon enough, all of us was out in the pale light, walking the path along the Cheat River to chapel. It was an angry stretch of water, too dangerous for wading and no good for fishing. On a windless night we could hear it from our dormitory, whispering with menace, threatening any hope we had of running away. I picked up a rock and threw it deep into the trees, longing to hear a rich thunk of it landing in a patch of still water. I didn't hear anything but the rush of the river, as if she was laughing at me. I threw two more rocks just to mock her back. *Oh yes I will,* I told her. *I'll leave this place someday.*

CHAPTER TWO

I Frighten THE SNAKE-HANDLING PREACHER *and* MR. BEADLE, THEN I TELL RUFUS A SECRET

By the time the sun filled the chapel, the preacher was deep in his sermon, and everything about us was a sin. Copperheads and rattlers coiled round both wrists, and he was slogging back and forth, telling us we was destined for hell. He was a rickety man with a curved back and bent knees. His cheeks were sunk from all the teeth missing in the back of his mouth. Talking about our sins filled him with energy. He went on and on, huffing and puffing like he was putting out a fire.

"And those that's filled with envy, and those that's filled with wrath, and those that's born to debtors and thieves and the wanton—all of you sitting here is halfway to the Devil. . . ."

"For land's sake, can't we do nothin' right?" whispered Rufus. "I can't help it if my daddy's in jail." Like me, Rufus's mother was dead, but he knew where his daddy was—locked in the jailhouse for stealing a ham.

"Nope," I whispered back, "seems like we was sinnin' the moment we was born poor."

The preacher started calling boys up to the altar so they could see how the snakes warn't daring to strike 'cause he was filled with righteousness. First he called up Meek Jones, the humblest, scar'dest boy at the orphanage.

"Meek's 'bout as sinful as a daisy," whispered Rufus.

"I'd like to see him call Walter Barnes," I whispered back, rolling my eyes at the thought. "He'd kick those snakes right outta his hands."

Well, I should've known to keep to myself in church.

The preacher's eyes were roaming the aisles, and he managed to glance my way just as my eyes was rolling in my head. He thought I was talking to a spirit and giving him the evil eye. He staggered back like I'd hit him with a pole.

"Lord in Heaven!" he called out, trembling in front of the altar. "There's one among us conversing with a demon! Right here in God's house!"

Well, the snakes started rattling and hissing because of his own nervousness, but the preacher didn't realize that. "Don't do it, Billy Creekmore!" he called out. "Don't tell these serpents to strike me!"

Next thing you know, Mr. Beadle stomped over to me. His switch was out, and he was all set to save the preacher by beating me outta my bad intention. Fortunately, my mind started ticking, and my mouth filled with words. Just in time, I stumbled out to the aisle and fell to my knees, lying my head off, and calling out for everyone to hear,

"Oh, please, dear Lord, take away this evil spirit! It's tellin' me awful things! It's set to harm the preacher here in your church! Oh, please, take it away!" I waved my arms about and dropped my head like I couldn't bear seeing what was before me.

Well, if I told you my act managed to stop Mr. Beadle in his tracks while getting every set of eyes and ears glued on me at the same time, I would not be lying. Everyone thought they were witnessing someone fighting off a spirit and talking to God. It was silent 'cept for me, and I was halfway between believing myself and laughing out loud with the power I felt. This time, storytelling saved me from the switch, and I was right relieved.

Naturally, the service took a turn after that, and nothing went along in the usual way. Somehow or other the preacher pulled the snakes off himself without being bit, then he started praying over me with Mr. Beadle himself dropped to his knees. The boys sang some hymns for my soul while I knelt in the aisle acting pious and remorseful. Up by the altar, the snakes were coiled in their little wire box, hissing so loud you could hear 'em in the silence between hymns.

For a while I was singled out and special, even if it was for being purified of a demon. On the walk back some of the boys drifted behind like they was afraid, while some clustered around me like I might help 'em see visions of their own. No one stepped on my heel or sent a rock singing my way, which are just two of the things boys did when a grown-up wasn't looking.

But it didn't last. An hour later I was just another Appalachian orphan at the Guardian Angels Home for Boys, the charity farm for the sons of the wayward and the dead, doing Sunday chores. Some was repairing the fence and some was cleaning the pigsty. It was a mean-spirited little farm, dreary and run-down. All the farm animals were angry and fierce, nothing cuddly or cute at all. Chickens pecked us, and geese nipped our heels. Barn cats darted out from bales of hay just to hiss and scratch at the air when we passed. The haggard old mule stared at us from his stall with dull eyes.

"What'd that ghost look like?" asked Rufus. It was early afternoon, and we was spreading straw on the barn floor. "Seemed to be awful threatenin'."

"Oh, he was handsome! Wore a top hat and carried a watch chain. Looked like he was a millionaire when he was alive."

"How 'bout that!" he said. "Wonder why such a good-lookin' spirit would want to harm the preacher?"

"He didn't say," I replied quick, hoping he'd drop the subject. Honestly, pretending to see spirits could be an awful burden. I didn't want to be dishonest with Rufus, but I didn't know how to get out of the lie. Plus, it was hard to explain. I sensed spirits, but I didn't see 'em. It warn't nothing like what I went on about in the chapel. It was altogether different from my storytelling, which I could tap into any time I wanted. I didn't have no control over sensing spirits.

"Maybe the spirit don't like the way the preacher tries to scare us to Heaven with his snakes."

"Bet you're right," I said.

The cows started mooing and stamping, turning to glare at us with their great moony eyes. They didn't like talking.

On our way outta the barn, Rufus and I put down our pails of milk to give the mule a pat. "One night, Rufus, you and I are gonna ride this mule outta here. He's gonna take us to a new life away from the Beadles and the preacher."

Rufus scratched him under his chin, and his eyes almost flickered with pleasure. "I don't know, Billy. This mule is awful beaten down. Why, he don't even have a name."

"Well . . . ," I started. I couldn't hold it in any longer. "I know someone goin' off to a new life. This mornin' I heard Mr. Beadle tell Peggy that one of the boys was leavin' with Mr. Colder tonight to apprentice in his factory."

"Is that the truth? Well, I wonder who it could be?"

"I'm bettin' on Walter Barnes," I said. "He's gettin' so nasty, I'm thinkin' Mr. Beadle would like to get rid of him."

"You could be right," Rufus replied. "But it seems to me he's too big. I think Willis would take to the work better." Rufus had such a grown-up way of talking. He was awful smart for a little boy. Didn't seem to be growing none but kept up with his reading and writing better than anyone else at the orphanage.

The rest of the day went by dreary and slow. We painted and weeded, repaired and swept. At the end of the day, we was glad to sit down to eat our supper. A few of us stayed behind afterward, drying plates and wiping pots, listening to Peggy tell us about the circus she saw in Albright last year.

"It was grand, boys, grand! Trick riders and acrobats, and a tableau of Roman statues! The actors were painted white from head to toe, and they were so still in their poses, you thought they were made of marble instead of flesh and blood."

"Imagine!" said Rufus, his eyes bright with wonder.

We all agreed it seemed like a fine life—traveling and performing and making up new acts to dazzle folks in your spare time.

Just then an automobile came up the road. It was Mr. Colder. All of us boys ran out and cheered him, waving our caps so he'd blow the horn for us. It was the only automobile we ever saw, and it was terribly exciting. He sounded the horn a few times for us, then waddled to the porch to shake hands with Mr. Beadle.

When the two men disappeared into the house, some of the boys dared to climb in the car and sit in the seats. I watched 'em take turns sitting in the driver's seat, pretending to drive off. Who was gonna be the lucky one? I wondered. They was happy as could be, turning the wheel, and inspecting the hood ornament. Pretty soon Peggy came onto the porch and scolded us for touching what warn't ours.

"I'm warning you! Mr. Beadle will be coming out here in a moment! Making such a racket, you are! Someone'll be getting the switch for sure!" No one paid attention till she stomped her foot, then off they scattered, and the lot of us went to bed.

CHAPTER THREE

I SPY

on the Dinner Party

and

HEAR MR. BEADLE

Tell

TWO LIES

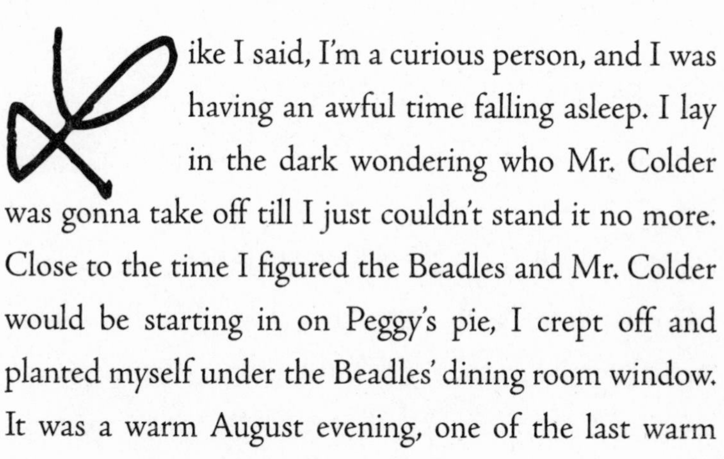

Like I said, I'm a curious person, and I was having an awful time falling asleep. I lay in the dark wondering who Mr. Colder was gonna take off till I just couldn't stand it no more. Close to the time I figured the Beadles and Mr. Colder would be starting in on Peggy's pie, I crept off and planted myself under the Beadles' dining room window. It was a warm August evening, one of the last warm evenings of the year, and the moon was full and bright. The window was open, and when I looked in I saw Mr. Colder stuffing his face.

"Mrs. Beadle, your pie would win a prize at any fair."

"Why, thank you, Mr. Colder," she said, blushing away. "I do take pride in my baking, but no more than virtue would allow." I couldn't believe she was pretending she baked that peach pie!

"Dear Mrs. Beadle," Mr. Colder went on, "I certainly hope you do not waste your talents on the miscreant boys in your charge! It would do them more harm than good."

"I quite agree, Mr. Colder," she said. "Do you know, at first I felt quite badly about serving them the dry bread and thin soups that we do. I thought it was unchristian to keep them so hungry and thin. Time has taught me differently. Now I see them in a clearer light."

"As we all do," said Mr. Colder. "We were naive when we first came across this class of child, weren't we? Thought they needed love and education, warm food and a comfy bed, didn't we? How wrong we were! Oh no, it's work they need! Work and a spartan life are the only ways to elevate them to a nobler stature."

On and on they talked about what we needed to better ourselves. Then Mrs. Beadle excused herself, and the men got down to business.

"I need a quick boy," explained Mr. Colder, "one who can move about in the close quarters of the furnace room."

Peggy bustled in to clear the dessert dishes, but Mr. Colder waved her away.

"I believe I have just the boy for you, dear Mr. Colder," said Mr. Beadle. "He's well coordinated and smart enough, but there's one slight problem."

"What could that be?" asked Mr. Colder. He leaned back in his chair, arching his back so that his big belly nearly bust his shirt.

"His age, Mr. Colder. I can't be certain, but I think he is only ten."

"Perhaps you've misread his birth certificate. Or maybe you've lost it?"

"These things are so difficult to keep track of,"

moaned Mr. Beadle. "We've had so many boys come and go."

"Difficult work you do, Beadle," said Mr. Colder in a most respectful voice.

"Thank you, Mr. Colder. Your words are most gratifying. And you, sir, you too are providing a great service to this class. You give them a chance to make an honest living so they won't repeat the mistakes of their parents."

They were so full of congratulations for each other, I almost got sick.

Mr. Colder cleared his throat, getting ready to say something awful important.

"Now, back to this boy you speak of . . . The most important thing for a boy in the glassworks is speed. I need an agile boy who's quick on his feet! By the time a boy is eleven or twelve, he's too old to learn the trade! His body's too big and clumsy. The breakage and waste the bigger boys incur is intolerable! I have to deduct the breakages from their pay or else I'd never make a profit. No, the government is shortsighted. Most boys of eleven or twelve are just too old. And it's a loss, a loss for them!"

"Right you are, Mr. Colder."

"So, about this boy . . . perhaps he's merely small for twelve. Is there any documentation for the boy? A record of his baptism? A birth certificate, perhaps?"

"Come to think of it," said Mr. Beadle in a most solemn voice. "I believe his records were lost in the flood. When the river overflowed two years back, a box of records stored in the cellar was washed out."

I couldn't believe my ears. What a bald-faced lie that was! There warn't no flood to speak of.

"Very well then. I'll pay you the usual fee if he's successful. A month will tell."

"I'll ask Peggy to get him ready to go. His name is Jones, by the way, Meek Jones."

Off Mr. Beadle went to fetch Peggy. Mr. Colder stuck his finger in the side of the pie and licked it. He was leaning back in his chair, patting his big belly, when I left. I heeled it back in the dark and slipped into my cot.

Soon enough Peggy came in with a little knapsack for Meek. She bundled up his things and told him he was off to learn a trade, and warn't that a fine thing, and that Mr. Colder was waiting to take him away in his motorcar. She made it sound ever so bright, but I thought I heard her voice catch, and I wondered if she warn't holding back a few tears.

CHAPTER FOUR

I Predict SOMEONE'S DEATH, RUFUS STARTS A CLUB, *and* AUTUMN BRINGS A LONG, COLD RAIN

"We was both wrong," I told Rufus Twilly soon as he woke up. I nodded to the empty bed. "It was Meek Jones."

"But he ain't twelve," said Rufus, rubbing the sleep outta his eyes. "He won't be till next year."

"I know. Mr. Beadle said he didn't know exactly how old he was. Told Mr. Colder a flood washed away his birth certificate."

"That's a lie plain as day," said Rufus.

"Seems Mr. Colder pays him a fee for findin' a good worker."

"For Heaven's sake!" said Rufus. "How do you know?"

"I went spyin' on them last night. Hid under the dinin' room window and heard every word they said. I'd have asked you to come, but you was sound asleep."

"Well, wake me up next time!" said Rufus. "I like spyin' at night."

I told him I would.

The day progressed normal. Mr. Beadle warn't in the dining hall for breakfast or lunch so we said our prayers sloppy and quick. Peggy slipped us extra biscuits and second ladles of soup. Geese nipped, cows kicked, and barn cats hissed. After lunch Mrs. Beadle, all cranky and creased in her face, gave us our lessons in the cellar. She wrote the names of the presidents on the blackboard with her squeaky chalk and made us copy 'em down. She was an awful teacher, but, to be fair, I don't think a better one could have made a lesson stick. We was too worn out for that, 'cept for Rufus. He was focused as could be, taking care not to let his ink spill and writing slow in his composition book. I let my mind wander, thinking about what lay beyond the mountains surrounding the orphanage and generally enjoying the coolness of the room.

Before we left, Mrs. Beadle called me over. She had a new postcard from my pa, the first one I had since Christmas. She dropped it in my hands, then scurried away, like she was too afraid to let her fingers touch mine or look too long in my face. There was a picture of George Washington on the card, a drawing of a statue in a park surrounded by flowery trees. All the boys wanted to see it, for we hadn't ever seen but one other picture of him, the one Mrs. Beadle had hanging in our little classroom in the cellar. The words were written in blue ink—"with love from your pa" it said, as usual. I let the boys pass it around, feeling ever so mournful as I watched it go from hand to hand.

Why my pa sent these cards, I couldn't say. If he thought they'd lift my spirits, he was sorely wrong. On the hill above the chapel was the little graveyard where the boys that died of pneumonia and measles lay buried. I looked at the crosses, wishing I could do more than just sense spirits, wishing I really could talk to the dead. Maybe they could tell me why my pa didn't come get me, or if my mother forgave me for causing her death. Perhaps the spirits knew why he didn't just forget me entirely instead of sending me a card every now and then. It was shameful knowing that my pa was alive but didn't want to raise me.

Back in the dormitory I put the card in a little tin box I kept under my cot. Inside were a dozen others, and the only thing I had of my mother's—a broken string of beads. They were blue glass, frosted with gold and white. When I was younger I used to think they looked like planets.

Mr. Beadle was back by supper, leading us in our blessings and overseeing our table manners. He made Walter Barnes leave the table before he was done eating for slurping his soup and boxed another boy on the ears for burping. He was revving up to give some boy a whipping, and all of us were getting pretty tense, especially Rufus, who tended to hiccup when he got scared. I could hear him stifle a few, so I pushed him under the table where there'd be less of a chance Mr. Beadle would hear.

As we trudged back to the dormitory, I felt cold air from the river sinking into me. The day was ending fast and autumn was on its way. Soon we'd be wearing our jackets all day, even sleeping in 'em, for we didn't have more than a thin blanket on our beds.

Up ahead some of the boys were throwing stones into the woods. A bird cried out.

"Say, Billy," Willis Dawson called out, "what's that whippoorwill saying?"

I had convinced the boys that my powers with the dead included understanding birds, since everyone knows they're the messengers between the living and the dead. I put a yearning look on my face and raised one hand to my chin. Boys stopped throwing stones and gathered round, waiting for me to talk. The sadness I felt ever since receiving my pa's card was disappearing, and I could feel a story coming on.

"It's sayin' someone we all know is gonna die soon. . . ." I stared off into the distance like I was all consumed with translating what I heard. "And it says . . . not to worry none, for it's gonna be a merciful death that'll put an end to sufferin'. . . ."

"Maybe Mr. Beadle's gonna die." Walter Barnes smirked. "That'd put an end to my suffering." He took aim at the broken branch of a box elder and let a stone fly. It reached its mark with a sharp cracking sound. Walter was a good shot, and in general, I stayed out of his way.

"Is Mr. Beadle gonna die, Billy?" asked Frank Vickers. "Where'd we all go if Mr. Beadle dies?" Even I was getting the cold shudders from standing in the near dark talking about death.

"Whippoorwill don't wanna say who's gonna die," I said. "He only says not to worry none, 'cause, like I said, it'll be a merciful death. He says everyone should turn round to the left three times, then spit on the ground to ward off any evil spirits lurkin' about."

Even Walter Barnes, brash and hard-hearted as he was, turned and spat. No more birds cried out from the woods, and it was too dark to throw stones, so we turned in for the night.

Weeks passed, and late summer became autumn. Leaves turned colors, then crinkled up and fell. Before it turned winter, a long, cold rain came. The paths got muddy and the river swelled. During the day we worked at shoveling mud outta the barn and laying down straw. Mrs. Beadle was having more and more of her spells, what with the wet weather and the short days, so there warn't no lessons to kill the time before lunch.

One gray day when the rain stopped for a bit, Rufus came up with the idea of starting a club. He marched us into the woods and made us sit around a rock.

"This here's the Robbers Club," said Rufus to the circle of faces. "Everybody that wants to join has to take an oath and mix his blood on this here rock. All the members must swear to stick to the club and never tell our secrets to no one; and if anybody does somethin' to anyone in the club, he must be banished and all members must swear revenge. Whoever hunts that person down has to bring back his scalp to this here rock. Then we'll have us an honor ceremony and cut a scar on his cheek and name him a warrior."

Everybody was willing, so Rufus pulled out his pocketknife and squeezed the top of his middle finger plump and jabbed it till a drop of blood came out. He smeared his blood on the top of the rock and told all of us to do the same. We passed the knife and mixed our blood, serious and quiet like we was in church.

"Do we always have to kill the people?" asked Frank Vickers.

"Oh yes," said Rufus. "It's best to do so."

"What's the business of this club?" asked Willis Dawson.

"Robbin' and stealin' so we can meet ransom if one of us is kidnapped by pirates."

At this Walter Barnes let out a snort of disgust and left since he didn't have no tolerance for games about pirates. Killing and scalping didn't make no difference to him, but he couldn't stand anything like pirates or life in the olden days that come straight from books.

Rufus went on talking about the clubhouse we were gonna build off in the woods and how each of us had to scavenge something in order to become a full member. It could be an animal pelt or a hawk's feather, an arrowhead, or something washed up on the riverbank, but whatever it was we had to find it on our own without no help from anyone in the club. He said we had a week to find something to contribute, then we adjourned our meeting.

For some reason, everyone but me was having luck finding things. Willis Dawson found a turtle shell, and Rufus found a dead falcon. He cut off the talons and fixed one set on a string to wear around his neck like an Indian and donated the other to the club. I walked everywhere with my eyes to the ground looking for flint or a rock with a vein of crystal, but I warn't having no luck at all. Once when I was milking the cow, I thought I saw a blue butterfly wing, but when I cleared the straw it was just a piece of broken glass. Daylight warn't proving any good for me, so I promised myself I'd try searching the next night with a full moon. Things turn up in the moonlight.

CHAPTER FIVE

A Voice Cries Out, and I Do My Best to Help A RUNAWAY *in* *THE MIDDLE OF THE NIGHT*

The full moon warn't more than a few days later. I waited till everyone was asleep, then I took a wander out behind the dormitory, thinking that maybe I'd find a snakeskin draped across a fallen branch. Puffy clouds collected here and there, then stretched thin across other parts of the sky. I headed off through a clump of bushes and slinked between trees. Wind rustled the bare branches. I searched in the tree roots, but I warn't feeling lucky. I was ready to turn back, when all of a sudden, somebody jumped out from the bushes and grabbed me around my neck.

"Don't yell or I'll kill you, I swear I will," cried a terrible voice. He was yelling in a whisper, and if you've ever been attacked at night, you know what I mean. "Do you promise not to yell? Do you promise? If you do I'll let you go."

"I promise," I said, choking out the words.

"Okay then. Now, put your hands on your head and turn round slowly."

I did just what he said, but when I turned around and saw who it was I couldn't help breaking my word. It was Meek Jones, and he was holding a broken branch in one hand like he was ready to hit me.

"For land's sake, Meek!"

"Billy!" he said, dropping the branch. "I didn't know it was you. I wouldn't have grabbed you like that if I'd a known. Don't hold it against me none. I'm awful desperate." The moon come away from the clouds and poured some light on us, just enough for me to get a good look at him. He was ragged and bone thin, and his right hand was wrapped up in a dirty bandage.

"Why, what's happened to you, Meek? You look like a beggar."

"I expect I am a beggar. I got burned. I lost most of my hand in the glass factory." He unwrapped some of the bandage for me to see.

Oh, it was awful! There warn't nothing left of his fingers but little stumps covered over with thin shiny skin. "How'd a fire do that?"

"It warn't a fire that burned me. It was molten glass. The boy next to me dropped the rod he was blowing, and melted glass splattered on my hand. Now I can't apprentice no more, and the only job I'm good for is sweeping the floor."

"Does it hurt you?"

"Oh, yes. It throbs and burns something terrible, but they don't care. I'm no use to 'em now, since I can't learn to blow glass with one hand. Why, they won't even let me sleep in the boardinghouse with the rest of the boys since I'm not making enough money to pay for my bed. They make me sleep on the factory floor. There ain't no future for me there, Billy, so I run off. I ain't got no money or food, so I thought I'd come here first and see what I can take from the kitchen."

"But you've been workin' there over three months now. Didn't you save up any money?"

Meek shook his head, staring at the ground. "No, Billy, it ain't nothing like we thought. You got to buy your own blowing rods, then pay for your bed and your meals. And, if you break anything, you pay for it. Seems like all you do is break things when you're first learning. At least I did, especially since it's so hot and crowded in the furnace room. Plus, after a couple of hours of staring into the furnace firing the glass, my eyes wouldn't see right. It seemed like I was going blind, so I bumped into people and dropped my rod and broke things. If you're lucky you make sixty-five cents a day, but once they deduct the price of your meals and bed and your breakages, all you get is a few pennies. The factory took all the money I saved up to pay for the doctor when I got burned. So, I ain't got a penny, and I'm hungry. . . . You'll help me, won't you, Billy?"

"Why, sure I will, Meek. You slept right next to me

for almost five years. 'Course I'll help you." I told him it was best if I went alone, since it'd be overall less noisy if only one person raided the kitchen. "Besides, I know it real well. Go hide among the willows and I'll head over there when I'm through. I'll hoot like an owl and you hoot back till we find each other."

The door to the kitchen was locked, but I lifted a window easy enough and climbed through. I put a wedge of cheese, some apples, and a loaf of bread in an old cloth sack. It had long straps and I figured it wouldn't be no hindrance for Meek to carry it across his shoulder. I looked around a bit more and added a bottle of apple cider and one of the dry sausages that Mr. Beadle ate for his lunch. I moved quick and steady, as if I was used to breaking into places and stealing every day of my life. It occurred to me that Meek might need a knife and some money, so I took one of Peggy's carving knives, and looked behind some cans in the pantry where I knew she hid a little pouch of money to pay the delivery boys. I felt a pang of guilt when I dropped it into the sack, for I knew Mr. Beadle might yell at Peggy or beat one of the boys when he found out he was robbed. But I figured that Meek needed the money more than anyone else right now. He looked so scrawny, and his hand was something awful to see.

I left quiet as I came, then ran toward the river. I hooted a couple of times and Meek hooted back, and sure enough we met up fine. He just about grabbed the sack of food outta my hands, taking big bites of the sausage and cheese and washing 'em down with the cider. He used the wrist of his injured hand to help him hold things on account of his fingers were too maimed to use in any way at all.

"You're awful hungry, Meek," I said.

"Yes I am." He wiped his lips with the back of his good hand. "Mr. Colder keeps us even hungrier than the Beadles." He reached into the sack and pulled out the pouch of coins. "What's this? Money? Land sake's, Billy, you're a wonder!"

"I thought you could use it. Where you headin'?"

"Don't know. Thought I'd follow the river a couple a miles into Albright. Maybe I could get a job in a store. I'm no good at fine work anymore. Can't see myself ever being much of a carpenter, which is something I used to think I'd like to be, but I can still sweep and clean and haul things about. . . . I tell you, Billy, the glassworks is a terrible place, even worse than here."

"I believe you, Meek. I've never known you to lie."

"And I ain't lying now. It's awful work. The furnaces are so bright, I heard they'll blind you by the time you're twenty-five. And they don't give you no water or breaks in the fresh air. You could faint away from heat exhaustion, and the foremen don't care. I seen a boy die there once. He hadn't worked there for more than a week, and it made him sick. He was vomiting blood all night and died the next day."

And then Meek dropped his head and started shaking like he was crying, but no sound came out, and there warn't no tears. He stopped soon enough, then got up and slung the sack of food across his shoulder. "Tell the other boys what I said about Mr. Colder and the factory. Tell them I said anyone who's sent there should figure out someplace to run off to soon as they can."

I told him I would. Then I wished him good luck

and told him to mind himself along the river. The current's dreadful rough in some places. I watched him slip into the willows, and the last I saw of him was the white sack I gave him. I could see a tiny bit of it between the trees, faint in the dark like a moth.

CHAPTER SIX

I Share Some Secrets

AND

Keep Others

Locked Up

WHILE MR. BEADLE

LOOKS FOR A THIEF

All night I tossed and turned, waking up every so often, once from a bad dream I couldn't remember, another time because of rain. I thought about telling Rufus and the boys in the Robbers Club about Meek Jones and his mangled hand, but I couldn't see no sense in that. The more people that know a secret the more likely it is to get out. If Mr. Colder and Mr. Beadle found out he'd been here, they might set out to bring him back to the factory and the horrible life he was leading there. No, I couldn't tell no one about Meek. The rain drummed on the roof like a thousand tiny mallets, and I don't think I ever truly fell back asleep. Near dawn I heard Walter Barnes let out a yell. Water was coming through the roof, and he woke up cold and wet from rain falling on his face.

The path to the dining hall was ankle deep in mud. For the first time ever, there warn't no bowls or spoons waiting for us when we took our places at the table.

"I wonder if Peggy's sick," whispered Rufus. A few boys muttered complaints, but those that noticed Mr. Beadle staring at us nudged 'em to silence. There he was, glowering at us and slapping his hickory stick against the wall, priming it for a beating. Right then and there my heart shriveled up, for I knew what he was mad about.

"Look at them, Peggy!" He pointed at us with the switch, his brow wrinkled with anger. "The most ungrateful lot of boys it has been my misfortune to know. Hungry, are you, boys? Well, there'll be no food, not a crumb for any of you, until the thief comes forward! Isn't it true, Peggy? Isn't one of these boys a thief?"

"Oh, sir, I can't say it's one of our boys. . . ." answered Peggy. "Maybe a tramp broke in last night and took the things. . . ."

"Most unlikely! No, no, it's one of these wretches, for sure. Tell them what's missing, Peggy!"

"One of my best knives, sir, some cider and a sausage, and a wedge of cheese . . ."

"And what else, Peggy?"

"Money, sir."

"Money!" he thundered. "Someone has stolen money from the Guardian Angels Home for Boys, the very hand that feeds him!"

Well, I wasn't sure if I was gonna faint or be sick. I felt right panicky as he stomped about. I longed for the earth to split open and swallow me whole, for in another moment I was sure I'd do something to give myself away. I sneaked a glance at Peggy, and her eyes sent me a fierce warning to stay silent, and I could tell she warn't gonna give me up to Mr. Beadle.

"I demand to know," thundered Mr. Beadle, "who stole from this orphanage?"

Nobody said a word.

"I warn you, thief, I will find you out! I will not let you steal from the good work of Guardian Angels. Until then, there will be no food for any of you! To your chores then, the lot of you!"

Out into the rain we scurried to tend the animals and shovel the mud. We worked for hours in the cold and wet, hunger gnawing at our bellies while Mr. Beadle patrolled among us, trying to unnerve someone into confessing. I was pumping water at the well when Peggy appeared on the back porch and pulled me quick into the pantry.

"Did you do it, Billy? You're the only one that knows where I keep the money."

"No, Peggy, it warn't me," I pleaded. "But I know who it was. . . . You see, I was awful restless last night, so I took a little stroll, and what did I see creepin' about the place but a convict! An escaped one, dressed in black and white stripes, limpin' through the mist with an iron on his leg."

"Stop it, Billy! Now tell me the truth. Is it you that stole from the kitchen?"

I swallowed the rest of the lie, then told her the

truth. "Yes, it was me, but I have a good reason . . . it warn't a convict, it was Meek Jones. He'd run away from Mr. Colder's glass factory, and he was hungry and injured, crippled really. He won't ever be able to use his hand again, on account that it was almost burned off by melted glass. . . ."

I described his accident and how pitiful his hand looked, and in a few short moments, Peggy's good heart prevailed, and her anger went away. She scooped me up in her arms, hugging me tight, as she cried for poor Meek and his crippled hand.

"Oh, to be a poor hungry orphan, cold and injured wandering alone in the depths of night!" She cried a bit more, then added, "Next time you come across a hungry, injured child you wake me up. I could have put together some money and food without Mr. Beadle ever noticing it was gone. . . ."

I assured her that next time I found myself in such a situation, I'd do just as she said. Then she let me go, but not before cautioning me about the state of my soul and decrying the bad habit of lying I had developed. "It will get the best of you in the end, for you'll get too easy with words. You're taken by the power of storytelling, and if you ever use it to hurt others, you'll be lost, Billy." Her face was pink with emotion, and I thought she might start crying again, but she didn't. Instead, she told me to slip back among the boys while she figured a way out of this mess.

For the rest of the day I tried looking as innocent as I could, but inside I felt troubled. My mind was full of the secrets, and I was so possessed by them that I barely felt the rain falling on my face. All day long I heard the river roaring. It was swollen and angry from two days of rain. No doubt the bank would be slippery and wet, and the narrow path that wound between tree roots and boulders was probably buried in dark water. I thought of poor Meek Jones making his escape with his sore hand, and I hoped he had decided to walk some other way than along the river.

CHAPTER SEVEN

THERE IS NEWS OF MEEK JONES,

and

on Hearing Plans for My Future,

I BEGIN TO BELIEVE THE PROPHECY

of

Bad Luck in My Life

All of us went to bed hungry that night, hoping that a night's sleep would change Mr. Beadle's resolve, but this was not to be. We warn't given nothing but weak tea for breakfast, then Mr. Beadle sent us to our chores. For an hour or so he paced back and forth on the porch, sheltered from the rain, while he watched us getting colder and wetter. Finally he left, but it hardly made no difference since hunger and rain had taken the spirit out of everyone.

Sometime late in the afternoon, Mr. Beadle marched us into the chapel. Already I was nervous. We never went to chapel except for Sundays, and I was sick with dread, figuring that Mr. Beadle had decided to hold us there until one of us confessed to stealing from the kitchen. But I was wrong.

In front of the altar was an open pine coffin holding the body of Meek Jones. At first all I could see was his profile, but I could tell it was him. My heart went cold, and all I could hear was the blood thumping in my ears.

Using his preacher voice, Mr. Beadle announced that the thief had been found. It was none other than Meek Jones, former resident of Guardian Angels, who was found drowned not a mile downriver, his body tangled in the roots of a willow, his head battered against the rocks. Around his neck was a white sack filled with stolen food and money, testimony to how God punishes those who steal from the hand that feeds 'em. The boy had run away from the glassworks factory, broken into the kitchen at Guardian Angels Home for Boys, and was on his way with the stolen goods to who knows where. Evidently, Meek had lost his footing along the riverbank, but whether he was first dashed on the rocks and knocked unconscious or strangled to a faint by the straps of the sack before he drowned, only God could say. "But let this be a warning to you boys, that your earthly acts determine the course of both this life and your everlasting soul, and if it were for me to determine, I would say that he was strangled by his sin."

The grown-ups were gathered near the coffin at the front of the chapel. The preacher was there, as was Mrs. Beadle, Peggy, and Mr. Colder, standing behind poor Meek. Mr. Beadle called for each of us to walk past the coffin to see what can happen to a boy who lies and steals and runs away from his responsibilities. Until then, I must confess, I was feeling greatly relieved knowing that I'd never be caught and the blame was thrown on someone else. But seeing poor Meek made me feel most dreadful and sick. His face was terribly swollen from the water, and the bandage around his maimed hand had fallen off. Mr. Beadle and the others were very solemn and stern. They stared at us with cold faces, as if we were somehow to blame for Meek's thievery and bad luck. Only Peggy was crying. She dabbed at her eyes with her apron and couldn't raise her face to look at us as we walked past the open coffin.

The preacher called upon us to look deep within our souls to humbly ask God to make us eternally grateful and forever worthy, so we'd never repeat the sins of Meek Jones. Then he gave one of his long-winded prayers asking God to forgive Meek for his many sins and wash him clean in the flames of Purgatory so he could rise up to Heaven. The way he put it, such a thing was unlikely, seeing what a low-down sinner Meek was. Afterwards he lead us in a hymn, and back we went to the dormitory, Mr. Colder and Mr. Beadle flanking us, Peggy and Mrs. Beadle bringing up the rear.

"So it was Meek the whippoorwill was talking about!" said Frank Vickers.

"I guess so," I answered, wondering if spirits really were starting to infiltrate my storytelling. It was just part of my story, not even a guess or a true feeling, and it turned out to be true. I was feeling right spooked at myself, and I wondered what kind of powers I really did have.

"Did you ever think it was gonna be Meek? And who'd have ever thought he was a thief?" said Rufus Twilly. The lights were out, but all of us was restless with the terrible vision of Meek and the sad end he came to.

"Makes sense to me," said Walter Barnes, sour as usual. "Once he stole a biscuit from the tin under my bed."

"Can't say I ever saw that side to him," replied Willis Dawson, who was the only one who could stand up to Walter, for they were the same size, although Willis warn't near as tough as Walter. I stayed out of the conversation for fear I'd spill out all my secrets if I started talking. So I made out like I was going to the privy, and out in the dark I went.

Gusts of wind rattled the trees, making the branches toss their arms about as if they was wild. Clouds pulled apart leaving patches of black sky sprinkled with stars. I stuffed my hands in my pockets, hunched my shoulders, and walked into the wind. At first it felt good to be alone, but then the wind stopped blowing, and I could hear the river rushing and gurgling over the boulders.

This was the last sound Meek ever heard, only it was all around him, roaring and accosting him, filling his mind and pulling him under. Soon enough, the sound of the water was filling me, and I felt certain Meek's ghost warn't resting peaceful. Maybe he blamed me for what happened to him since I gave him the very sack that weighed him down. Maybe it strangled him when he fell into the river. I tried cluttering my mind by humming so I couldn't sense Meek's ghost or hear it trying to talk to me. I walked back to the orphanage away from the woods.

Across the way I could see that the lights were on in the Beadles' dining room, so I crept on over to my spying window.

There was Mr. Colder and Mr. Beadle sitting across from each other. Each had a piece of pie, but neither was eating. It seemed that they were arguing about something. I leaned toward the window, close as I dared, and tried to hear what they were saying.

"No, Mr. Beadle, your offer is unacceptable. I cannot pay for the boy's coffin and burial and then offer you a fee for providing a new apprentice. The company lost money on Jones as it is, and now we need another boy to replace him. I will not pay you the usual fee in this instance. I want you to provide me a new boy free of charge."

"Be reasonable, Mr. Colder!" yelled Mr. Beadle. He banged the table with his fist and made the dishes clatter. "I have agreed to allow the boy to be buried here, thus saving you the cost of transporting the body to the paupers' graveyard near Charleston, but surely you don't expect Guardian Angels to pay for his coffin and burial?"

"I do indeed expect it, Mr. Beadle! I do so because you lied to me when you first discussed him. You said he was a compliant boy, sharp-witted and nimble, a boy who could be easily trained. He was so clumsy, he got himself maimed and then cost us the doctor's fees. . . ."

They went on and on, arguing about who would pay for this and why the other owed that. It was easy to see Mr. Colder was going to win the argument. His voice was loud and firm, but overall he was less excitable than Mr. Beadle. Eventually they came to an agreement. Mr. Colder would pay for the coffin but not the gravediggers, and Mr. Beadle would provide another boy to apprentice in the factory without taking the usual fee.

"And who will you be sending?"

"His name is Billy Creekmore, a bright boy, a very capable boy, but quite meek at the same time. . . ."

It felt like I'd just been struck by lightning. The cold shivers descended upon me, and my heart started thumping.

"Very well then, Beadle. Our disagreement is settled. I'll come for the boy in a week," said Mr. Colder. You could tell he was pleased as punch with himself. He shook his head and smiled. He picked up his pie and ate it with his hands.

Somehow or other, I made it back to the dormitory. Don't ask me how, 'cause I don't remember. I didn't have to look deep in my heart to know that I couldn't survive life in the glass factory. The heat and the noise of the furnaces seemed like hell itself, and I knew for a fact that Mr. Colder wouldn't pay no attention to my stories 'bout seeing spirits. He was a rich man who warn't about to pay for the coffin of a poor boy who worked for him. Seemed to me he'd be comfortable speaking to the Devil himself. My heart started aching, longing for my pa to come fetch me. I was in a terrible fix. What happened to Meek Jones could just as soon happen to me, and I had to figure a way to escape.

CHAPTER EIGHT

DREADING AN APPRENTICESHIP *IN* THE GLASS FACTORY *I Plan* MY ESCAPE

Two days later, early in the morning, some men came to dig Meek's grave. There were three of 'em, and they was already working when we filed into the dining hall for breakfast. Meek's grave was on the highest part of the hill, and the sound of their shovels striking the earth filled the little valley. Rufus and I watched 'em while we drifted through our chores, three faraway figures under a bare oak.

"Ain't it bleak, Billy?" asked Rufus.

"Sure is," I answered. Two of the men were resting with their backs against the tree while the third kept digging.

"Has Meek been talkin' to you? Is he mournin' 'bout being dead?"

"He's awful sad to be dead," I said, thinking back to the night I wandered by the river and was too scared to hear his spirit talk to me. It was on the tip of my tongue to unburden myself to Rufus. I wanted to tell him how I was the one who gave poor Meek the very sack that made him drown, and how scared I was that his ghost was out there, waiting to wreak its revenge. But I couldn't tell him without burdening him, too, so once again I buttoned up.

Before dinner, in the last bit of pale light, we gathered in the graveyard to pay our respects. Meek's pine coffin looked awful small resting there next to the big dark hole in the earth. The skinny old preacher led us in some prayers, and then Mr. Beadle and the men grabbed the ends of some rope and lowered the coffin into the grave.

"Good-bye, Meek," I whispered when I threw a handful of dirt on his coffin. "Please don't haunt me none when I run away at night."

For the next few days and nights, the only thing I could think about was running away before Mr. Colder came to get me. If I took the river path, I expected I'd meet up with the ghost of Meek Jones, so I figured the road to Albright was the best way to go. No doubt it'd be the first place Mr. Beadle would look for me, so I'd have to hide somewhere during the day and make my way at night. Where I'd hide during the day, I couldn't say. I never heard talk of any caves or hideouts along the road, no barns, or shacks. For the first time ever, I realized just how plain ignorant all of us boys at Guardian Angels was. Why, most of us had never been anywhere 'cept the general store to help Mr. Beadle carry a load of lumber and sacks of feed. No wonder we were all so eager to go off with Mr. Colder to the factory in Morgantown. We was thinking we'd be seeing the world. Only I knew different now, and the truth of what went on was scaring me so bad I couldn't sleep at night.

So there I was, tired and scared, my mind racing,

hoping the first snow wouldn't fall the day I had to leave. I did my chores and kept to myself. I was so glum, Rufus Twilly thought for sure I had received a card from my pa.

"Where's he now, Billy? Ain't he sendin' for you yet? It must be awful sad knowin' that your own pa don't want nothing to do with you. At least I know why my pa won't come get me. He doesn't get outta jail for another three years. . . ." He chattered on, but I wasn't really listening. *If only my pa really would send for me,* I thought.

We were gathering eggs in the chicken coop. The hens was squawking about, and their reddish feathers were floating in the air. For the first time ever I noticed they were the exact same color as the freckles all over Rufus's face. It made me laugh out loud.

"Rufus, do you know your freckles are the same color as these hens, which is the same color as your hair. . . . And your skin's as white as their eggs." I was laughing so hard, I was doubled over. A few of the eggs in my basket fell to the ground and broke.

"Well, you don't have to tease me 'bout it, Billy! I

can't help it. It's just the way I was made."

I was laughing so hard, I lost my breath. When it came back I said, "I don't mean to tease you none, Rufus, it's just that I never noticed it before, and it struck me funny, probably 'cause all I've been thinkin' about is Meek and what happened to him."

Meek's name caused Rufus to ease up, and he warn't angry at me no more. "Sure was a terrible thing that happened to him, warn't it, Billy? But maybe God was punishin' him for stealin' from us. . . ."

"I don't think so, Rufus," I said. "I don't think God wants us to suffer the way poor Meek did, no matter what he did."

All of a sudden, I became powerful worried about Rufus. Why, in another year or so, Mr. Beadle might sell him off to the factory.

"Listen to me, Rufus, I'm gonna tell you somethin' and I want you to remember it. Don't ever let Mr. Beadle send you off to that glass factory. I can't tell you how, but I know it's a terrible place. It ain't like they tell us. There ain't no adventure or fortune or fun of any sort there. If you ever get word that it's your turn to go, you gotta run off. Start figurin' out where to go and how to get there *now*. And don't tell the other boys what I said. Remember what I'm sayin', you hear me?"

"Yes, Billy, I hear you. I can't say I understand you, but I hear what you're sayin'."

"Good. You don't have to understand. You just remember what I'm tellin' you now."

Rufus and I gathered the rest of the eggs without talking. We covered up the broken ones with straw, and I fell into a dark mood again, worrying that I had said too much and not enough at the same time. I didn't have more than three days to figure out what I was gonna do. If only I knew how to get word to my father. Surely he'd come get me if he knew what lay in store for me.

Gradually, it began to occur to me that I should tell Peggy about my plight. After all, I reasoned, she told me I should have woken her up the night I saw Meek so that she could help pack him some food. Why, she might even help me make my escape and get word to my pa that I had moved on. I was thinking about how she walked to Albright every Sunday to go to mass at the

Catholic church. Maybe I could sneak in with her so she could point me in the best direction for running away once we were in town. There must be other roads besides the one going into Morgantown.

"Are you sure it was your name Mr. Beadle gave him?" she asked. "You were awful scared that night. Maybe you didn't hear right."

I assured her I heard right.

"Why they're nothing but slave traders, they are! Trading away the lives of poor motherless boys!" Then she picked me up and rocked me awhile, crying at the sadness and injustice of it all. Once she set me down, she was all business, and we worked out the beginnings of my plan. Peggy would put together a little sack of food and get me some money. There was only one road into Albright from here, and three roads out. She didn't know of any hideouts along the way, but once you crossed the river, you were on your way to Fairmont, a town almost as big as Morgantown. Peggy would take me to the road herself and get back to her church in time for mass, same as she did every Sunday. We'd have to be careful to make sure that no one saw us together, but seeing how she rarely ever saw a soul else walking into Albright early Sunday morning, she warn't too worried about that.

In the meantime, I started getting ready to leave. I put my few possessions in an old flour sack that Peggy had given me. I packed some socks, my tin box of postcards, and my mother's broken necklace. Once I was set up in another town, I'd write Peggy a letter pretending I was somebody else so she'd know where to send any postcards my dad might send.

At times I'd get right excited about my new life. Why, I could change my name, if I wanted, and make up a story about how I came to Fairmont and what I was seeking. I'd say I was brought up in a holler down the way, and all my kin had just dropped dead of fever, and that I came to town to make a living and learn the ways of city people. I didn't bother thinking up too much detail, since I figured I'd have plenty of time to make up my story once I struck out on the road.

Other times I'd get bogged down by worries. What if I lost my way? What if the snow came early and I didn't have any shelter? What if my father came to fetch me before I was settled somewhere? Then Peggy couldn't tell him where I was, and we'd be lost to each other forever.

"For Heaven's sake, Billy!" yelled Rufus. He was tired of me staring into space and not hearing him "What's wrong with you these days?"

"Oh, nothin'," I lied. "I can't stop thinkin' 'bout Meek."

"Poor Meek! Warn't it awful, Billy?"

"Sure was," I answered, feeling sadder still, for I realized I'd probably never see Rufus again and he didn't even know it.

Soon enough it was Friday, my next to last day at Guardian Angels Home for Boys. I ate breakfast and went about my chores feeling both heavy in my heart and excited at the same time. None of the animals seemed particularly mean that day. The cows didn't kick and the geese didn't nip. Mrs. Beadle was in the kitchen when we came in for lunch, looking almost healthy, although I'd have to say she was still the wrinkliest, skinniest person I'd ever seen in my life. She was helping Peggy pass out bowls of soup to us. I took mine and said thank you, and I was almost feeling good at my place in the world, until I heard her say something to Peggy once my back was turned.

"He's here now," she said. "For Billy."

I near crashed my soup on the floor. I turned to look at Peggy, but I didn't catch her eye, and I didn't hear what she said back to Mrs. Beadle. All I could think was that all our plans had gone to waste, and I was off to the glass factory for sure.

The next thing I knew, Mr. Beadle was stamping into the room. Behind him was a little man with his cap in his hands. He hobbled in, doing his best to keep up with Mr. Beadle but having trouble doing so, for one of his feet was turned inward and he had to walk on the side of it.

"Creekmore!" he yelled. "Billy Creekmore, get over here, boy!" For a moment I thought I should just push past the two of them and make a run for it out the door, but I was too shocked to act, so I did what I was told. I stood before the two of them trembling with fear.

"Do you know this man, Creekmore? He claims to be your uncle!"

"Oh, he don't know me, sir. Never saw me, but I'm his uncle, honest to God, husband of his mother's sister I am. I have a letter from the boy's aunt explaining how we came to know he was here, if only you'd take a look at it, sir. T'is here in my pocket. No reason I'd lie about a thing like that." He had a soft, musical voice. "Don't be afraid, lad," he said. "I'm here to take you to live with your aunt Agnes and me. We want to care for you, which is what your poor dear mother would want, God rest her soul."

CHAPTER NINE

A SURPRISING LETTER Starts Me on *a New Life*

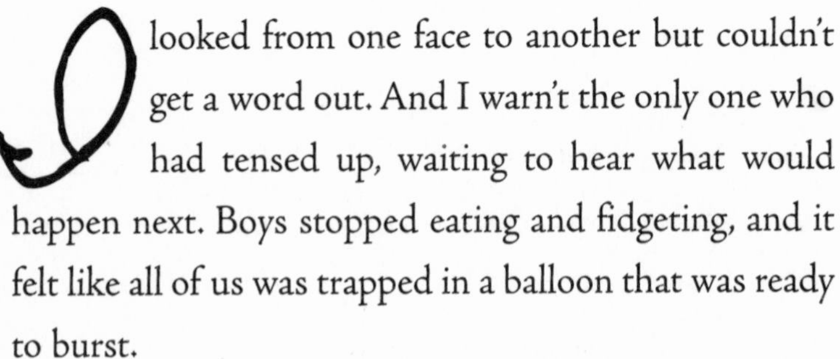

I looked from one face to another but couldn't get a word out. And I warn't the only one who had tensed up, waiting to hear what would happen next. Boys stopped eating and fidgeting, and it felt like all of us was trapped in a balloon that was ready to burst.

"A letter?" Mr. Beadle sputtered. "I will, indeed, see this letter! Hand it over at once!"

"Oh yes, sir. I'm glad you're taking a look at it, for it's sure to answer all your questions," said the man. "I'd be happy to read it to you, sir, for the handwriting's hard to figure in parts."

"I can read it just fine!" glowered Mr. Beadle. He took the pages out of the man's hand and began to read aloud.

Dear Sir,

My husband, James Berry, and I have heard that a ten-year-old boy named Billy Creekmore is in your care. We believe this boy is the son of my sister, who died shortly after he was born. Only recently have we learned of his existence. His father, also named Billy Creekmore, wrote us when my sister died and said their son was stillborn. Last month, however, I heard news that leads me to believe that he wasn't telling the truth and that the boy is alive. I was tending the bed of a sick woman in a mining camp not far from our own, when I heard the story of an unusual boy near ten years of age named Billy Creekmore. The teller of the tale, a healing woman like myself, claims she delivered the boy at midnight on Friday the 13th, 1895. The boy's father abandoned him shortly thereafter. She took care of the child for a while, then left him at the Guardian Angels Home for Boys, an orphanage run by her cousin and her husband. Knowing that the name and age of this boy match that of our nephew, should he indeed be alive, my husband has come to see him. If the boy no longer resides with you, we appreciate any help you might offer in determining his whereabouts. If he does, we thank you heartily for caring for him up to now. We are his only living relatives and wish to raise him as our son.

Sincerely yours,
Mrs. James Berry

"Are you Mr. James Berry?" thundered Mr. Beadle, to which the man answered yes, he certainly was. "And do you have a birth certificate? A baptism record? I need documentation, my good man. It's the only way to determine if you have claim to this boy."

"No, sir," said the man sadly. "We didn't know he existed. How could we have such things? I can tell you, though, that he has the same sort of chin as my wife and her sister, and the same blue eyes with black lashes. And he's the right age with the name of the man we know to be his father."

"Sir, this is not good enough, not good enough at all! Until you can prove you are indeed his next of kin, I am his legal guardian, and I have arranged for him to be apprenticed to the glassworks factory in Morgantown."

"The glassworks!" gasped the man. "Surely you wouldn't send him to a life as miserable as that!"

"It has been arranged. The boy is going to the glassworks."

"But, sir," pleaded the man, "I'm telling you, sir, as I look on him now, I know he is my wife's one and only nephew. If only she were here beside me, you could see for yourself. And if the likeness is not enough for you, sir, could you please find it in your heart to let go the matter of a baptism record or birth certificate? All we want is to offer the boy a home."

All of a sudden, Peggy stepped forward. She was heaving with crying, tears streaming down her face. "Why don't any of you ask Billy what he wants? Surely his voice counts for something."

Mr. Beadle was too shocked by her insolence to say anything. He stood there with his mouth open, glaring at all of us. I took advantage of his silence to say my piece, my head tingling as if I was making up the biggest lie I could, only this time it was the truth.

"Please, Mr. Beadle, I want to go live with my uncle."

Mr. Beadle fumed with anger. He reached in his pocket and pulled out a little gold magnifying glass. He held it up to one eye and looked over the letter here and there, what for exactly I couldn't say. I imagined he was double-checking the part that mentioned his wife's cousin, the healing woman, for surely that was something he couldn't ignore. The letter must have looked sound enough, for he gave it back with nothing more than a sigh. Paper was paper, and he wasn't up to fighting it, especially since he spent so much time lying about things like birth certificates and letters. So, he had to let me go with the man I came to call my uncle Jim.

Well, I was near bursting with questions, such as if he knew where my father might be, and what my mother was like, but things got all in a rush and I had to be patient. Uncle Jim waited in the kitchen with Peggy while I gathered my belongings and said good-bye to my friends. I had been delivered from the glassworks, by an uncle I never knew I had. Inside I tossed between soaring happiness and feeling stunned by the strangeness of it all. It was easy enough to get my things since I had packed them all in the flour sack days before, but it was harder than I thought to say good-bye. I never thought I'd have to do it, since my plan was to sneak away while everyone was sleeping.

"So, off you go, eh, Billy? Will you ever think of us?" asked Walter Barnes. I could hear the jealousy in his voice, and I knew it warn't any kind of question I could answer without making him even angrier than he already was.

"Of course I will. I'll even write you from time to time."

"Sure you will," said Walter with a smirk. He didn't believe me, and I felt guilty knowing that I probably wouldn't write Walter, or anyone except maybe Peggy and Rufus.

"I'll write you," said Rufus. "You know how good I am at writin'." His face was so earnest and shiny, it made my heart sad. "Write me soon as you can with your address so I can write you back."

"I will," I said to him, turning away before he could see my eyes tearing up.

I carried my tin box and my bundle of clothes and met up with my uncle. Peggy's voice was happy and bright for she learned he was from Wales, which is just across the sea from where she was born. She smiled and shook his hand again, telling him that she loved me like her own little brother.

"Be a good boy and mind your uncle. I can tell he's a kind man. Where's your home, sir? How far do you and Billy have to go?"

"We live in Holly Glen, miss, twenty miles southeast of Charleston. Not so very far, but the mountains here in West Virginia make every journey a long one. We'll take the train there, for it's too far and rugged for our old mule to travel."

"The train! How exciting for you, Billy! What a glorious thing! Oh, be happy, Billy, for you're with family now and there's an adventure before you as well!" And with that she scooped me up for one last hug in her great arms. She cried a little, and I did, too, for I knew that Peggy was always and forever my true friend, the likes of which I might never find again.

And so I turned my back on Guardian Angels Home for Boys, walking the same way I had planned for my escape, only now I was leaving with an uncle I didn't know I had, and with a home waiting for me in a faraway town. Bare branches reached across the narrow road to each other. The ragged Cheat River tumbled below without a threat to be heard. It was the first time I remember feeling steady in the world, even though I was walking with a man I barely knew to a faraway place I didn't know. The woods seemed to be whispering good-bye to me. "Good-bye," I said back to 'em, and if Uncle Jim thought it was strange, he didn't say so.

Part Two

CHAPTER TEN

My Uncle Jim and I Get to Know Each Other *as We Travel* *to* Holly Glen

There warn't no need to hurry, since Uncle Jim was slow for an adult on account of his bad foot. It had been near crushed in a mine cave-in years ago. "But it doesn't slow me down in the mines, and I can still shovel ten tons of coal a day, as good as any man and better than most. Now take me hand, lad, since we're coming up to the town and the streets are crowded. I couldn't bear to lose you."

If there was a bigger city in the world, I couldn't imagine it. Albright was busy with folks out shopping and taking a meal. The store windows was filled with all sorts of things like sleds and folded dungarees, galvanized pails and a whole set of brushes for clothes and hair and who knows what else. We made our way to the train station at the far end of town. We sat on the benches near the tracks, and he offered me a sandwich from his lunch pail.

"It's a ham sandwich with a bit of cheese," he said, "made by your own aunt Agnes for you." He opened a bottle of cider to share with me.

I near ate it whole since I was hungry enough to faint. I was getting used to his musical way of talking. It was almost like Peggy's, but softer in the way he said his *r*'s and more lilting.

"Did you know my pa?" The question must have surprised him, for he didn't answer right away.

"No, lad, but your aunt did."

"Why'd he write you I was stillborn?"

Uncle Jim shook his head. "I can't speculate, lad, and I don't want to pass judgment on another man."

"Did you know my mother?"

"Yes, lad, a kind woman she was. Not as strong-willed as your aunt Agnes, nor as practical. More disposed to fancy, I'd say, always seeing the good in the world."

We ate the rest of our lunch in silence. I didn't know what else to say, so I was quiet. Uncle Jim gave me a piece of apple pie that Aunt Agnes had baked special for me. I licked the crumbs off my fingers, wondering if I'd always eat so good from now on. I hadn't had pie in a long time. A few people waited with us. Some had suitcases, some had nothing more than a bindle and a sack. Before too long the train came, screeching to a stop with great puffs of steam spreading over the platform.

"Settle in by the window, Billy. Soon the mountains will be rugged and beautiful, and you'll enjoy the view. We won't be getting to Holly Glen until tomorrow morning, for we have a long wait at Charleston. But don't worry. Once we're there, we won't have to walk far like we did today, for all us miners live along the tracks."

Soon enough the train pulled out of the station, and the town of Albright was swallowed in the distance.

The rhythm of the tracks made me drowsy, and I drifted to sleep, glad to be warm in the train and not on the road trying to find shelter.

I can't say much 'bout Charleston or its train station. I was sound asleep when we got there. Uncle Jim steered me to a different platform to wait for the train to Holly Glen. We sat on the bench, and he let me sleep against him till the train came. "But I want to see the station," I said, even though I couldn't keep my eyes open. Uncle Jim hushed me, saying it's best to get my rest and not to worry none. There'd be other chances to see Charleston and the station.

"I'll take you to the circus when it comes to town," he said. "A grand circus it will be. You'll see the station then, and the town, too."

The circus! In my mind I heard Peggy talking about the trick riders. I fell back asleep dreaming of them galloping around the big top.

Dawn came and so did our train. I was wide awake by then. I pressed my forehead against the window, trying to look into the houses of the mountain towns that hugged the tracks. We stopped or slowed for each little camp we passed, letting passengers on or off, or just taking a pause at the depot. Most were mining camps, said Uncle Jim, named after the owner's wife, like Holly Glen, which Mr. Newgate named after his wife. The coal company owned all the buildings we saw, as well as the land beyond the mountains. It was the same in Wales, he said.

"I went to work in the colliery alongside my father when I was eight. I moved here to West Virginia when I was twenty, for the mine was near empty by then. Mr. Newgate sent a man to our village, promising free transport to America, and a good wage to anyone willing to work in his mine. And so I came to Holly Glen, where I met your aunt Agnes, who ran the boardinghouse where I first lived, cooking and doing laundry for us miners."

He turned his hands over for me to see the coal dust that filled the lines of his palms and stained his fingertips. It couldn't ever be washed away, no matter how long and hard he scrubbed. Some of the dust was from Wales and some from here. "And some is from the hands of me own father from when he first helped me learn to walk, I'm sure."

"Will I work with you in the mines? Like you did with your pa?" I asked.

"Not for a while, lad, although there's boys as young as you working as trappers or spraggers. But they're from the big families with five children or more. Or else the father's been killed or injured, so they need the money a boy can make to pay rent and buy food. But it's dangerous work, Billy, not fit for a young boy unless the family is desperate. There's those that are, but not your aunt and me, thank Heaven."

"But I'd like to work in the mines," I said.

"Thank you, Billy, but my wages pay for what we need. Besides, I have a plan for you. I'd rather have you work as a mule driver. Why, eventually, when you're near twenty, and if you're good, you'll make more money than a miner. All in all, it's a better job, one that you can take with you out of the mine if you wish."

"How do I learn to do that?"

"You'll have to work our mule, Coppers, learn to take him around the town with a wagon. It's harder than it sounds, for a mule has a mind of its own. Until then, your aunt will be pleased to have you around the house.

There's plenty to be done at home. Tell me now, did you have much education at the orphanage?"

I described our lessons with Mrs. Beadle, how my friend Rufus took to them just fine in spite of how boring they was, but how I just couldn't keep my mind still enough for anything to sink in. "Mostly it was Bible stories, copyin' and recitin' things we memorized from the chalkboard. I'm pretty dreadful at it, Uncle Jim, so I don't mind workin' with you in the mines."

"No, lad. Mining is harsh work. I've seen too many boys brought out crippled or dead. Best to stay in school for as long as you can, for the miners that can read survive the work better. They're less likely to turn to drink for ease from the hardships of their work. Give me a nice fire and a book by Mr. Charles Dickens instead of whisky," he said. "Drink can ruin a man's character and make him beat his wife and children. I've seen it in Wales and West Virginia both."

As we crossed a great steel bridge that traversed another river, a light snow began to fall. It clung to the trees but melted fast on hitting the tracks. At last we came to Holly Glen. Rows of wooden houses, their front doors facing the tracks, layered up the mountainside. Each chimney puffed a black curlicue of smoke, and a crowd of children stood in the middle of a dirt road, waving at the train. Behind them wandered two black and white cows. Far off, at the other side of the depot on its own street, was a grand house painted white with a porch running the length of it. Uncle Jim said the supervisor lived there.

He pointed out the window to one of the small cabins. "There's your new home, Billy! And look, there's your aunt waving to you from our porch! That's the way of her, Billy, already wanting to welcome you. A kind woman she is. She'll be walking to the depot now, I'm sure, for she can't wait to see you and hold you in her arms."

CHAPTER ELEVEN

I Meet MY AUNT AGNES, *Learn a Bit About My New Home,* and MAKE A FRIEND

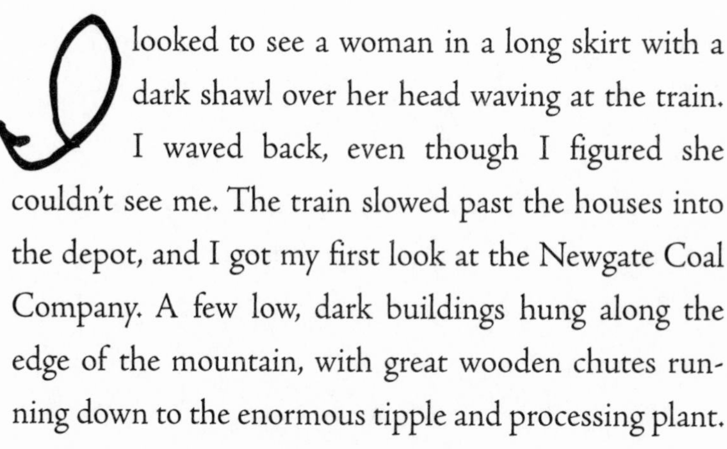

I looked to see a woman in a long skirt with a dark shawl over her head waving at the train. I waved back, even though I figured she couldn't see me. The train slowed past the houses into the depot, and I got my first look at the Newgate Coal Company. A few low, dark buildings hung along the edge of the mountain, with great wooden chutes running down to the enormous tipple and processing plant.

These was the tallest buildings I'd ever seen, and they was gloomy black with coal dust. A separate track split off to run under the tipple, and a mound of spilt coal was built up on one side. A little girl was climbing it, and she was black all over with soot. Even the tips of her hair was black.

"Take off your cap, lad," said Uncle Jim as we stepped to the platform, "for that's showing respect for a lady, and here comes your aunt Agnes."

I took off my cap as did my uncle to greet her. She bounded across the platform with long, fast strides, unafraid of slipping in the snow, one hand closing the shawl at her chin. She was nearly a foot taller than Uncle Jim, with a straight posture and rather hard features. Her clothes was perfectly neat and simple, as if frills of any sort might slow her down. She carried a gentleman's gold watch.

"Well, now, here you are!" She gave me a tight, short hug, then held me at arm's length to get a good look at me. "Look at his eyes, Jim, just like May's. How is he? Is he a good boy?"

"Oh yes, Agnes, pleasant company he was on our

long trip. Well mannered and eager to please."

"Isn't that lovely, Jim? Oh, but he's lanky, probably restless, too. It goes with long bones. . . ."

"Now don't set too much in his shape, Agnes. You never know with boys. They go through many changes till they're grown."

"Well, yes, right you may be. . ." For some reason I had disappointed her. Maybe she remembered how I killed her sister, or maybe she knew about my habit of spinning tales. I shifted my feet and turned my hat in my hands a few times.

Aunt Agnes pulled out her watch, then snapped it shut. "We must be off," she announced. "I want to warm you up by the fire before lunch. Otherwise the grippe might set in."

We left the depot, my aunt in the lead pulling me along by the hand, my uncle hobbling after us. By now the gray sky seemed to be splitting open with snow. It fell fast and thick, obscuring everything around me, covering the wooden sidewalks and the dirt road through town. We walked to the front row of houses and entered the one in the middle.

Aunt Agnes sat me in a chair by the coal stove in the center of the room and wrapped me up in two shawls. She pulled out a tiny brown bottle of something or other from her doctoring bag and rubbed it into the back of my neck. "Here's where the grippe sets in," she said. "Once it's in your throat you might as well go to bed, for sick you'll be a week or more at least."

"Oh, but your aunt is good with medicines and poultices," said Uncle Jim as I sat there all bundled up. "When folks can't afford the doctor they send for her, for she won't take money for her gift. She grows her own herbs, you know, and makes all her tinctures and syrups herself."

"Make him some tea, Jim, for we've got to warm up his insides, too."

"Yes, Agnes, here I go now, and aren't you a lucky boy, Billy! Yes, you are, a lucky boy!"

"I sure am," I answered, not knowing what else I could say. But in general I agreed with him and felt that I had finally fallen into some good luck. We drank our tea, and only after I insisted that I was truly warm inside and out did they let me unwrap and get out of my seat.

I wanted desperately to poke around a bit, like any boy in a new place would, but I didn't want to seem too restless or curious, for I didn't want Aunt Agnes thinking poorly of me. So I tried sitting still without fidgeting, doing my best to be polite. They asked me questions about Guardian Angels, such as was I treated poorly or well, did I have many friends, and did they learn us a trade, and so on and so on. It was all pretty tiring, but eventually they let me up to look around. They showed me the straw mattress where I'd be sleeping, the privy in the back, and the water pump down the road. They introduced me to Trotwood, their milk cow, and Coppers, their mule, and the flock of chickens roosting in the coop.

"I'm embarrassed to have you see the old barn," said Uncle Jim. "It's in awful need of repair."

I took a look and saw where some planks had rotted through and the gate hung crooked.

"Maybe I could help you fix it up," I said.

"Certainly, lad. I can use an extra hand."

We had beef stew for lunch, as much as I could eat, and it was rich and delicious, with plenty of meat and parsnips, potatoes, and such. Then a mob of children knocked on the door. There was six of 'em, all eager to meet me, having heard I was coming from far away to live with my aunt and uncle. All in all, they was even more ragged and scraggly than the boys at Guardian Angels. They pushed and shoved to get in the front when Aunt Agnes opened the door, but she quick took charge, making them quiet down and shake the snow off their boots before letting them inside.

"This here is Billy Creekmore," she said, "my sister's son. He'll have many stories to tell you about living in an orphanage and traveling a great ways to come live in Holly Glen. But for now, you may introduce yourselves, then be off, for I'm trying to spare him the grippe."

A girl in boys' breeches asked me how old I was.

"Near eleven," I told her. "My birthday's in December."

"You're tall, but awful skinny," she said. "Looks like you're half starved."

There warn't nothing to say back since it was true, so I kept my mouth shut.

"Well, don't go insulting him on his first day, Rachel,"

said a boy my size. "I'm Clyde Light and this here is my brother, Belton." A little fellow with great big eyes poked his face out then snapped it right back. "He's shy, but he wanted to come meet you, right, Belton? We live at the boardinghouse across the tracks with my ma. She's manager there ever since our pa died last spring. You'll have to come visit tomorrow since it's Sunday and there ain't no school."

The other children stood around to get a look at me till Aunt Agnes pulled out her watch and said it was time to go home. "That Rachel's a bold one," she said after closing the door. "Just like her mother."

Before long the sun was going down. Aunt Agnes took me to milk Trotwood. I gave her a try and she milked easy without kicking or turning her great face to moo at me the way the cows at the orphanage did.

"It does me good to have you here, child," said Aunt Agnes. "My heart's full in a way it hasn't been since May died."

"Was she pretty?"

"Yes, and she liked being told so. She was a romantic, always had her nose in a book. Do you read, Billy?"

"I can read some, but I'm not one for books. I can't sit still long enough to get through one."

"Neither can I, Billy. Long as there's work to be done, I'm up and about. Then I'm too tired to read."

By the time we was done, it was dark outside. The three of us sat down again for more stew, then it was time for bed. Judging by how quickly I heard snores coming from their room, I'd say Aunt Agnes had tired herself out. My straw mattress was lumpy in places, but I felt awful cozy. The coal stove was still warm from the day's cooking. I looked at the glowing embers through the grate, trying to get my mind around how big the day turned out to be. I tried to remember all the kids that came by, but the only faces I could put names to was Belton and Clyde. I wondered why my aunt was discouraged over my long limbs, and what would happen when my pa found out I was here instead of at the orphanage. Maybe he'd be angry at the Beadles for letting me go and making it harder for him to come get me. Then outta the blue I missed Peggy and Rufus so bad, I began to cry.

CHAPTER TWELVE

MY AUNT TELLS ME SOME ABOUT MY MOTHER *and* I ATTEND MY FIRST DAY OF SCHOOL

Sometime after I fell asleep, it must have snowed awful heavy, for when I woke up the mountains was white and the ground was covered. I swept the snow off the porch for Aunt Agnes and cleared a path to the road. Everywhere you looked, the snow was sprinkled with coal dust. I ain't never seen nothing like it. Specks was frozen in the ice and peppered the top of the drifts. It was a strange sight at first, but I got used to it. Near everything in a coal town is tinged with black.

It was Sunday, and toward the late side of morning, Clyde Light and his brother, Belton, came by to take me sledding. Clyde didn't have nothing more than a sheet of plywood with an axle fixed to it, but he said it sailed. We trudged through the snow to the sledding hill, which lay just past the last row of cabins. Clyde was my age and still in school, much to his shame. His brother, Belton, was going on six. Like Aunt Agnes and Uncle Jim, Clyde's mother was mad to keep him outta the mines long as she could, but Clyde reckoned he'd be going soon enough. Last year his pa got his legs crushed in a cave-in, then lingered in the hospital for near a month before he died. He left his family with a mountain of debt, which is why Clyde's mother ran the boardinghouse for the Russian men. Mr. Newgate let her keep enough money to care for Clyde and Belton, but took the rest to pay off the hospital bill.

"There's still an awful lot to pay off," Clyde said, "and a son can't let his mother work herself to death. Now, just take a look at this hill, Billy. We're gonna roar down it, I'm tellin' you."

There warn't a tree or stump or outcropping of rock to be seen. It was smooth and slick, glistening with ice clear down to the bottom, where it emptied onto a frozen pond. Clyde said that years ago the company cleared it to build a community hall, but they never got round to it. Kids was all over it, sailing by on sheets of cardboard and wood, or rolling down by themselves with their arms tucked in. One little guy was sitting on a pie plate sliding down the hill in slow, lazy spirals, giggling to himself.

I jumped on behind Clyde and yelled for Belton to get on behind me. But he just looked right through me like he hadn't heard and started twirling in place with his arms outstretched, talking to himself in a language all his own.

"Don't worry 'bout him," said Clyde. "He's happy. He'll do that till he falls down."

"Is he deaf?" I asked.

"No, he can hear fine. He just don't understand words. Don't use 'em either. Now, get ready, Billy, 'cause I'm fixin' to take off."

And with that Clyde dug in his heels and pushed us down the hill. We passed kids on cardboard and pie plates, whooping it up as we went over hard little drifts, then flew into the air for a flash. We smacked back down with a thrilling little thump of pain and managed to hold on till we hit the pond. We tumbled off dead in the middle of it, laughing our heads off and staring at the blank sky.

Things went on like this for hours, and I don't think I ever felt so happy and free in my life. Clyde and I took turns sitting in front of the sled. For the most part, Belton kept to himself, watching us from behind a tree or twirling about. Toward the end he went down the hill a few times on his seat, laughing like any other kid there. Finally, our clothes was damp, and bits of ice started freezing up our hair, so it was time to go. Clyde said he'd catch up with me on the way to school tomorrow, but I guess Belton didn't like that idea. He threw his arms around Clyde's waist and tried to drag him to the ground. Clyde yelled at him to stop it, that he was talking 'bout tomorrow not today, and that he warn't going nowhere right now but home with him.

"He hates when I go to school. Can't even stand me talkin' 'bout it," explained Clyde. "You'll see tomorrow." And then he told me to just go on 'cause Belton was acting up and overall he'd be easier to handle if he was alone with him.

When I got home, Uncle Jim was sitting by the stove reading his book and Aunt Agnes was sewing a torn shirt. She put down what she was doing and made me change out of my clothes. Once again she wrapped me up in blankets and had me sit by the fire while she rubbed her tinctures into me.

"You're a mix, you are," she said. She was working on my shoulders now. The smell of menthol was making me relaxed and sleepy. "I see both your parents in you."

"How so?"

"You're tall like your father, long-limbed and restless. But you've got your mother's eyes, and her heart, too. She was fond of people, understanding, and people liked her back. I see her in you, how you make room for Belton and don't cut yourself off from Clyde because he has a strange brother."

"Why would I do that?"

"Lots of folks do. Won't talk to Clyde or his mother for fear whatever ails Belton might rub off."

Belton was strange, more like a creature than a child, but he didn't frighten me. I thought about how he babbled to himself and wandered among the trees. "Do you think he communes with spirits?" I asked.

"Maybe."

I paused, debating whether or not I should tell my aunt about my talent with spirits, the very talent that killed her sister. But perhaps because she seemed to be seeing me, like no one else ever had, I did.

"I do. Sometimes they come to me."

"So I've heard. The healing woman says you talked to spirits the hour you were born."

"Folks say it killed my ma. Made her die from fright." I got awful jumpy inside. My heart was pounding. Maybe I was making her talk about something she'd rather forget.

"I don't know about that for I wasn't there," she said, "but lots of women die in childbirth, Billy. I've seen it many times here in Holly Glen. Just last spring I helped bring a baby into this world, only to attend the mother's funeral days later. I don't blame you for her death. May was always sickly. Had a weak heart from the host of fevers she suffered as a girl. I was all set to help her with your birth, but your pa's letter came the day I was planning to leave. He said you came early and was stillborn and that May was dead."

A wave of relief poured over me. Maybe my mother didn't die because of me. Maybe it was her weak heart. No one ever told me she was sickly before. At the same time I couldn't help wondering why my father had lied about me.

"Why'd he write you I was dead?"

"I have thought and thought about that, Billy, and I just can't say. All I know is that your pa was always secretive, elusive I'd say. He was never one to talk about his past or his plans for the future. He courted your mother off and on for two years, showing up on our doorstep with a present from one of his travels, then taking off again without a word of explanation. I held her hand while she cried over him many times."

"Why'd she marry him?"

"He made her feel alive. Made all of us feel that way.

He was handsome and charming, and he was always up to something exciting, like panning for gold in Alaska or traveling with a medicine show. When May first brought him to meet me, he took a dozen bottles of my tinctures to sell, but I never saw a penny."

I sat there silent, my mind filled with images of my parents, and the warmth of my aunt's tinctures working into me. I saw a man giving a pretty woman a necklace, then her waving good-bye. I saw a cabin in the woods and the same woman looking out the window for him and crying. My aunt was there with her, waiting for him to return. I sunk a little deeper in the chair while my aunt capped the bottles and put them back in her doctor's bag.

"All right, Billy, you're through. No grippe will be setting into you tonight."

My aunt's tinctures seeped into me, and I slept sound that night. I didn't stir until a loud screeching sound made me near jump out of my skin with shock.

"That's the mine whistle," said Aunt Agnes. She checked it against her watch then snapped it shut. "It's telling the miners they've got just an hour to get to work. Hurry up, now, so you can have your breakfast and walk your uncle to the mine." She told me she'd already been up for two hours, pumping water for the day and starting the stove, fixing our breakfast and packing our lunches. She timed herself regular, checking her watch as she finished one chore and started another.

The three of us ate breakfast at the little table by the stove, then bundled up for the walk through the snow. There was plenty of boys my age and younger going off to the mine, carrying the same tin lunch pails as the men. I carried one, with a pie baked in the top section just like my uncle's, though I was going to school. Some of the boys was so little they had to be carried on the men's shoulders through the drifts. The older boys nearly swaggered up the mountain. They called out to each other and laughed, while the ones just a year or so older was already serious as the men. I waved good-bye as Uncle Jim entered the mine, feeling like an awful sissy for going to school instead of the mine.

"In a year," said Aunt Agnes, reading my thoughts. "And not before. Don't you know why we walk our boys and husbands to the mine every morning? We might never see them again. Now here comes Clyde Light to show you the way to school."

"Mornin', Mrs. Berry," said Clyde, tipping his hat to her. Belton was dragging behind, holding his brother's hand and staring at the ground.

"Good morning, Clyde. Hello, Belton," she said. She glanced at her watch. "You boys better hurry. You'll be late." Then she was off, stepping in the footprints already in the snow so as not to get her boots any wetter than necessary.

"My ma says your aunt could run the mine," said Clyde.

"I expect she could," I answered. "Say, Clyde, see those little boys goin' up to the mine? What kinda job do they have? Seems to me they can't shovel no coal."

"They's trappers," said Clyde. "Spend the whole day sittin' alone by the ventilation door, openin' and closin' it for the mule drivers so the gases don't build up. It's how most boys start in the mines."

"Sounds dreadful lonely," I said.

"Oh, it ain't bad. It's the way you start. Now, look

smart, Billy, for we's at school. There's our teacher."

Miss Clark was waiting on the steps for her students. She shook my hand when I introduced myself and said she was pleased to have me. Belton started moaning soon as she opened her mouth. He clung to Clyde till he peeled him off, then Miss Clark closed the door. I stole a look at him through the frosty window, and he was red-faced with crying.

"Don't worry 'bout Belton," said Clyde as we took our seats. "He'll wander about the hills waitin' for us."

The schoolhouse was a little clapboard building with a coal stove in the middle and rows of desks all around it. It was right smart, I thought, for the inkwells was full and the pen nibs and pencils was laid out neat in the tray. Kids aged five on up to near twelve came in and took their seats. Rachel gave me a mean look. Only one boy seemed older than me and Clyde, which filled me with dismay. But Miss Clark seemed nice, and this cheered me up some. She was fresh-faced and young and moved her hands about when she talked. She introduced me to the class, then asked if I wouldn't like to recite something.

"Maybe there's a poem or speech you memorized in your other school that you'd like to share?"

"No, ma'am," I replied. And before I knew it, a story started coming on. "I'm not one for recitin', but I would like to say a few words, if I could, considerin' how I'm new to Holly Glen and don't know no one except my new friend Clyde Light over yonder."

"Why, certainly, Billy, that would be very nice."

"Well . . . ahem . . . ahem." I cleared my throat. "I just wanted to say how much I appreciate bein' here, seein' how all the boys I was raised with at the orphanage was such a low-down pack of thieves, dedicated to learnin' how to be pickpockets, robbers, and such. Some of 'em even started a secret club that was hell-bent on spyin' on folks at night and breakin' into their houses. The ringleader's name was Walter Barnes, and he was all set to make me join up, only my uncle, Mr. Jim Berry, saved me at the last moment by bringin' me here to Holly Glen. . . ."

"Please, Billy, your language! Hell is not a word for school, but still, I am very moved by your remarks, and we are very happy to have you here with us now."

"Thank you, Miss Clark, and sorry about the language." I took my seat and put my face in my hands for a moment, like I was tearing up with emotion. The class was silent.

Well, my little speech was a big hit. I wasn't just the new kid, or an older boy too sissy to work the mines. Instead I was someone who had seen some danger in the world, someone who knew pickpockets and thieves. They mobbed me at recess and pulled on my sleeves, begging for stories about Walter Barnes, whom I made out to be the meanest, strongest boy that ever lived. I had a grand time making up stories about him. I told the kids how he once threw a rock so hard it buried itself in a tree and how he took a copperhead right out of the hands of the preacher one Sunday morning and crushed its head. "He's not afraid of God nor man," I told 'em, and the younger ones shivered in their boots.

The rest of the school day was right interesting in its own way. Some of the kids spoke a strange kind of English, for their folks came from all over Europe to work the Newgate mine. There were kids from Wales, Romania, Italy, Poland, and Russia. It was a heap of fun hearing their accents and figuring out what they was trying to say, and all of 'em wanted to talk to me about Walter Barnes and his band of robbers.

"Oh, they was wicked thieves," I whispered to a corner of the room while Miss Clark wrote on the blackboard. "Used to roam about stealin' laundry off the line so they'd have plenty of disguises."

"Billy Creekmore!" Miss Clark spun on her heels. Her eyebrows was knitted together she was so mad. "You are becoming a distraction to the class!" If she warn't so nice and pretty, I'm sure I wouldn't have felt so bad. But since she was good-hearted and kind, nothing at all like Mrs. Beadle, I did my best to settle down. I got down to my lessons, working middling hard at my geography and spelling, and harder still at my numbers. I surprised her, 'cause I know my times tables all the way up to 6 x 7 is 44, but I told her I don't plan to go no further. I don't put no stock in mathematics.

Clyde said I did real well, considering it was my first day, and that he was proud to be my friend.

"What the heck do you suppose that ol' Walter Barnes is up to now?" he asked.

"Heaven only knows," I answered. "Still venturin' out at night and stirrin' up trouble, I reckon. I'm just glad to be away from him."

Belton was up ahead, hiding behind a tree, throwing little stones at everyone who came out the door until he saw his brother. He threw his arms around Clyde and clung to him all the way home, trying his hardest to put his tiny hand over Clyde's mouth when he spoke to me. He couldn't bear Clyde giving attention to anyone but him. Seemed awful irritating to me, but Clyde was used to it. None of the other kids could stand it, I guess, for the three of us walked home alone. Up ahead our classmates raced from one frozen puddle to another, stomping on 'em for all their worth and shattering the ice.

CHAPTER THIRTEEN

I Write Rufus A LETTER, *Start Learning* A TRADE, *and Receive My First* CHRISTMAS GIFT

ain't one for writing, but missing Peggy and Rufus bad as I did pushed me to do it.

Dear Rufus,

I'm living in Holly Glen, a tiny town between two great mountains with just a patch of houses, a store, a saloon, a schoolhouse, and a church. A man named Mr.

Billy Creekmore

Newgate owns it all. His picture hangs everywhere, even inside the schoolhouse just like he was George Washington himself. It's printed on the bills you get from the store and even on the scrip, which is how the company pays the miners instead of money.

School is tolerable, and overall I'm learning more from Miss Clark than I ever did from Mrs. Beadle. Still, I'm not cut out for sitting at a desk, so it don't count for much. I'm longing to work in the mine, but my aunt and uncle won't let me for another year.

Does the Robbers Club still hold meetings? How are Peggy and Willis? I'd ask about Walter but I figure he's mean as ever.

I was all set to write how we had twin brothers in town, one good and one bad, and how the bad one was always pretending to be the good one and getting invited into people's houses so he could steal their silverware. But Aunt Agnes was hanging over me and glancing at her watch. I signed my name quick and blew on the ink to set it dry.

A thin layer of ice covered the snow, and it made a delicious crunching sound with every step. Clyde came running along with Belton on his back, telling me how the annual Christmas party was just two weeks away. He was near breathless but too excited to stop talking.

"It's held on Christmas Eve, and the superintendent's wife decorates the church basement . . . and Mr. Newgate and his family come in from their big mansion in Charleston to celebrate with us. There's a Christmas tree and tinsel . . . and we eat a turkey dinner, and have the choice of yule log or pie. . . . Then St. Nick comes with a sack full of toys . . . and gives each of us a present."

"What sort of presents does he give out?" I asked. Seemed glorious to me since there never was presents at Guardian Angels. We stopped in our tracks for poor Clyde to take a rest. Belton slid off his back and started twirling with his arms outstretched, laughing out loud at who knows what. He never needed no resting at all.

"Last year I got a spinnin' top, and Belton got a train

whistle. Ma took it away from him as he was blowin' it night and day, waking up the boarders. He cried something awful. Pulled all the drapes down and shoveled ashes from the stove all over the floor. Made a dreadful mess and wouldn't stop cryin' for nothing. So I gave him my top, which calmed him down. Right, Belton? You like that top, don't ya?" Belton didn't answer. He was happy as could be, though, babbling and laughing to himself, off in his own world.

All day the sun was bright, so the ice melted. By the time we left school, the icicles hanging from the eaves were melting, and the roads through town were clear of snow. Sunlight fell in great shafts, and the shadows was dark and long. All over the village women was pouring great pots of boiling water into the tin bathing tubs on the porches. The miners would be home soon, and they liked to wash before entering the house. Clouds of steam rose up, billowed over the railings, and disappeared.

A few days later, my birthday came and I turned eleven. Aunt Agnes made me the first birthday cake I ever had—a little jam cake sprinkled with sugar—and we had Clyde and his family over for supper. The grown-ups gave me a toast with sherry and wished me many happy returns. They let Clyde and me drink the last little drops, but I couldn't see the fuss over it. It warn't more than a thin type of sugar syrup in my opinion, and why it deserves a little cut glass goblet I'll never know.

After Clyde and his family left, Uncle Jim led me outside. "It's time to try your hand with Coppers," said Uncle Jim. "Let's see how far we get before your aunt calls us in." His cheeks was bright pink from scrubbing, and his hair was wetted down and neatly combed. *My uncle's a gentleman,* I thought, *through and through.* Thick puffs of smoke rose from his pipe. We led Coppers out of his stall, and Uncle Jim showed me how to slip the bit into his mouth and hitch him to the wagon stored in the back of the tiny barn.

"He's cranky at times, for he worked long in the mines before I bought him, but eventually he comes around. Fix that buckle, Billy. You can't have that slipping if you want your mule to haul a ton of coal. Easy now. He'll kick if you startle him."

I bent down smooth and gentle and fixed the belt tighter. Old Coppers twitched his ears some, but otherwise didn't seem to mind.

"You should have seen Coppers the day he was retired! Like a colt he was! The driver led him out to the grass, and he trembled all over, like he couldn't bear the expanse of earth or the sun upon his back. Then he started jumping in place, gamboling and prancing about. Oh, it was wonderful to see. I bought him then and there from the mine and am happy to call him my own."

I patted Coppers's neck. It was warm and smooth and I could almost feel his blood coursing under his skin. I put my ear against him and listened to his pulse.

"Was Coppers a good worker?" I asked.

"Oh yes, one of the best. Visited ten different miners a day, picking up their cars of coal, leaving an empty one behind, then heading off to the weighing station. He could pull four tons of coal, he could!"

Uncle Jim puffed on his pipe. He seemed to be thinking things over, for he was nodding to himself.

"Aye, Billy, a mule driver is the best job in the mine. He moves around, seeing different people throughout the day, which is a good thing, for working alone in the dark gets lonely."

I led Coppers around the yard a few times, pulling the leads with a strong hand so he'd mind.

"But the best thing about it is that it's a trade that can take you places. A driver can work other jobs, delivering things for a company or working for hire. You could move out west or into Charleston. But a miner is stuck. He can only work underground, and it's a brutal life, one I don't want for you, lad." Uncle Jim gave me some raisins to give Coppers when we was through, then inside we went.

The next two weeks took their time, and it seemed like the holiday party would never come. But, finally, it was Christmas Eve. School was closed, the mine whistle didn't blast, and miners and kids got a holiday. We played in the snow, building snow forts and having snowball fights. Those with skates went skating on the pond near the tipple, and those with sleds sailed down the hill. Belton rolled down by himself, laughing at the sky, and spinning in circles at the bottom.

Just like Clyde said, the church basement was decorated for a banquet. Garlands of evergreen, ivy, and tinsel hung from the ceiling, and a huge Christmas tree with white candles and ornaments stood in the corner. The superintendent, the store manager, the doctor, and Mr. Newgate himself were all there. It was the first time I'd seen Mr. Newgate. He seemed to have gained a lot of weight since that portrait of him was made. He was rotund as Mr. Colder, with an even bigger belly and muttonchop whiskers. The lot of 'em sat on a table raised up on a little stage, eating with their families, as if we all wanted to look up at 'em like they was in a play. And they did look right nice, I have to say. They wore fine clothes, mostly made of velvet I'm sure, and the wives had dangling earrings and sparkly bracelets. The daughters had great big satin bows in their hair, and the sons wore waistcoats with starched collars. They looked just like their pas, only a little less fat and without the whiskers. At first it was quite a funny sight, seeing these little men, but then I realized we boys sitting below looked just like little miners. I figure it's just the way of things, how boys wear the clothes of their pas.

There must have been near a hundred of us in the basement, eating turkey dinner, and feeling toasty and warm. While dessert was being served, St. Nick came, only I knew it warn't really him on account of him being just a character in a story. I heard Uncle Jim laugh and tell Aunt Agnes it was the man who ran the saloon dressed up in a red and white suit with a fake beard. All the children ran to him and he commenced to passing out presents—jump ropes and tops, cloth dolls, jacks, slingshots, and paddleballs. Clyde and I got slingshots, and Belton got a cloth doll dressed like a soldier. He held it against his cheek for the rest of the night. We walked home full and happy, sleepy, too, from the full day of playing in the snow and all the excitement of the party. It was the first time I had ever had those feelings of being with family and friends, together and content, a good day behind us, another good day coming. There was never a moment like that at the orphanage, of happiness, safety, and hopefulness intermingled.

For Christmas, Uncle Jim and Aunt Agnes gave me

a whip, a proper one, too, not a toy. It was black and braided and ten foot long. It was a grand present, wrapped up in colored paper, with a string bow.

"You'll need to practice to work it right," said Uncle Jim. He took me out back and set up six empty cans in a triangle. He cracked the whip and knocked over the top one first, then the one on the left, then the one on the right in the second row. Then with the flick of his wrist and a loud crack he knocked over the bottom three all at once. I took a turn but didn't even get a decent cracking sound, let alone get close to the cans. Over and over I tried, but I kept missing and was snapping at air.

"Keep practicing, Billy, and eventually you'll get it. A mule driver can extinguish a flame without upsetting a candle. That's how much control a driver has with his whip."

That was all I needed to hear. I practiced regular—when I got home from school, after finishing my chores. On the weekends I'd practice morning, noon, and night, setting up cans and lighting candles, doing my best to perfect my aim and develop some style. I walked about the yard with the whip looped round my neck just like the mule drivers I saw walking home from the mines with the men. I didn't have the heart to use it on Coppers, though. He had too much of the whip for one life, I reckoned.

CHAPTER FOURTEEN

I Visit *a Grave* and *Receive a Letter* from *an Old Friend*

I didn't want to tell Clyde about my powers with spirits. I was off to a new start and didn't want folks thinking of me as the boy with strange powers. Being the boy with the dangerous past was good enough for me. Ever since I knew Aunt Agnes didn't blame me for my mother's death, I was happy forgetting what folks used to say about me. But Clyde was awful blue. The anniversary of his father's death was coming up. He didn't have no desire to go sledding or take any interest in my stories about Walter Barnes. He was even getting cranky with Belton.

"I'm tired of you!" he yelled, his eyes wet with angry tears. Belton had rushed him after school as usual, but Clyde pushed him away. "You ain't a baby! Go home by yourself and leave me alone!"

"Why, Clyde! I ain't never seen you like this."

"I miss my pa," he said. "It's coming up on a year since he died." He wiped his tears with his arm, but he was still choking on his words. "Everything's harder now. My ma works all the time, and some of the men at the boardinghouse is awful mean when they drink. I wish he was back. . . ."

Our classmates streamed past us, laughing and chasing each other home.

I took Clyde aside and whispered, "I'll tell you what . . . I ain't never told you this, 'cause it's cost me some trouble in the past, but I was born talkin' to spirits. Sometimes they come to me, and sometimes they don't. Maybe I could communicate with your pa's ghost."

Clyde was pretty unsettled with the news. He

looked at me like I said the sky was red, then he looked me straight in my eyes and said, "I could take you to his grave. Maybe he'd talk to you if I was there."

I said I'd give it a try, so we set off to the far end of town where the church was. Behind it, nestled between two low hills was the cemetery. You couldn't see it from the rows of cabins and boardinghouses where we lived. I guess Mr. Newgate wanted it that way, for nearly all the men and boys buried there had died in accidents in the mines. Underneath the snow was rows and rows of grave markers, all of 'em small slabs of granite. Clyde dug through the snow to find his daddy's.

"Here it is. The stone looks just like the day we buried him."

I knelt down in the snow and covered the carvings with my hands.

Wainford Light
1874–1905

The granite was rough and cold, for a miner don't get a polished tombstone. I quieted my thoughts and listened hard. At first, all I could feel was Clyde's grief and my own desire to ease his suffering. But gradually I began to feel something different. It warn't nothing more than the feeling you have when a bird flies overhead. But it was there, hovering above us, the first spirit I ever really felt. I used to think it would be a frightening thing, to really know a spirit was with you, yearning to talk, but it warn't. My heart beat steady and full, like it was growing inside my body, pushing out any other thoughts or feelings so that I was all over listening, like how a wolf or a fox or a bobcat listens with its ears and tails, whiskers and fur.

The spirit was sad and faint, and it didn't speak, but I put my own words to it.

"Your pa's not restin' easy. He wishes he warn't dead so he could raise you and Belton and be company to your ma."

"What else?" he asked.

I tried conjuring the spirit. I asked it to tell me what to say, but it was gone. I warn't gonna pretend otherwise. I couldn't take no joy out of deceiving Clyde.

"Nothin'," I said, "I don't hear nothin' else."

I don't know if it helped Clyde or not. He didn't talk

as we walked home. Gusts of wind whipped the ends of our scarves and pulled at our jackets. Low-hanging clouds was collecting over the valley.

"Looks like snow," I said. Clyde looked to the sky and nodded, but we was silent the rest of the way.

All day folks waited for snow, but it never came. We woke up to clear roads and another dull sky heavy with clouds. Later in the day, Aunt Agnes had me hitch Coppers to the wagon to pick up bags of flour and feed from the store.

By the time I loaded the wagon, a heavy snow was falling. You could almost hear the flakes hitting the ground. Coppers didn't like it one bit. He didn't do more than twitch his ears when I told him "giddyap," so I gave the whip a lazy crack. Just as I was about to flick it again, the manager leaned out the store with a letter in his hand. He was a fussy man who wore sleeve garters and an apron and kept his pencils sharp.

"Hey, you forgot your mail, boy! Didn't even ask for it. You'd never know you had some, if I didn't run after you."

"No, sir," I called back. "I plumb forgot." I jumped outta the wagon so he didn't have to walk in the snow to hand it to me, but he wasn't done scolding me. I listened and apologized, then thanked him for all I was worth until finally he gave me the letter. Well, my heart almost skipped a beat when I saw it, for it was from my old buddy Rufus. I tore open the envelope right then and there, and I would have stood there reading it, but the snow was almost as wet as rain, and the ink began to run. I stuffed the letter in my pocket, then jumped back into the wagon and cracked the whip. This time Coppers roused himself and trotted home.

No, wrote Rufus, the Robbers Club wasn't meeting, and, yes, Mr. Beadle was still a horror. Peggy did her best to slip 'em some extra helpings when he wasn't looking, and Walter Barnes had been sent off to the glassworks. He was happy to leave the orphanage, and, truth be told, the boys was happy to see him go, seeing how he was turning so bitter and mean. Things was almost pleasant in the dormitory with folks getting along for the most part ever since he left.

Your pa sent you a postcard and I told Mrs. Beadle I'd send it along. I passed it

> *around for the boys to look at, just like you used to do. Since there was a drawing of St. Nick on it and it being the Christmas season, I didn't think you'd mind.*

I looked in the envelope, and there was a postcard of St. Nick holding up a tiny Christmas tree with a star on top. It was a fancy card with scalloped edges and a bit of sparkle in St. Nick's beard and on the snow falling around him. The same words were there, this time in green ink.

"A card from your pa, eh?" Aunt Agnes was stoking the fire, warming the house for Uncle Jim. "He did the same thing to your mother. Sent her a card every now and then so she couldn't forget him."

I got out my tin and showed her the other postcards he sent me over the years. She studied the pictures some, but overall didn't seem too interested. Her eyes glittered when she saw the broken necklace.

"Why, I remember the day your daddy gave this to May! He bought it in a jewelry store in San Francisco on his way home from Alaska. He said it came all the way from Italy and was made of Venetian glass. The blue beads made him think of her eyes. Let me see, now . . ." She held the strand up to my eyes. "Yes . . . your eyes are the same color as May's."

She handed the necklace back to me. It was all I had of my mother, and I was happy to know it linked us in this way. Her eyes and mine was the color of the beads, and if my father ever saw me, he would recognize I was his son. When I put them back in the tin, I thought of poor Clyde and how he was aching for a link to his pa.

Snow fell off and on all week. One day it thawed and black slush lined the streets. Then it rained and froze again, so that all of Holly Glen was coated in ice. Drifts of snow was hard-edged and sharp with it, and whole trees glistened like they was made of glass. Clyde's mood lifted with the sudden freeze.

"I've got news for you, Billy Creekmore," he yelled at me. It was so slippery, we was skating to school on our shoes. "I'm off to the mine! Gonna start next week." The company was cutting his ma's wages since the boarding-house was only half full. A half dozen of her boarders had sneaked off in the night without paying their rent and left the company in the hole. There was a rumor saying they had gone to work in the Black Diamond mine thirty miles away, which was a bigger operation that paid better.

"So now my ma needs me to work, since she can't make enough money to feed the three of us and we still owe the hospital a lot of money. I'll be starting out as a trapper."

"I'm awful envious, Clyde," I confessed. "It's an important job."

On the morning of Clyde's first day, Uncle Jim walked him to the mine. His ma and Belton, Aunt Agnes, and I walked with them. Belton got all worked up seeing his brother go someplace other than school. He threw himself about, flapping his hands, then ran off trying to follow. Clyde shooed him away, but Belton kept running after him, throwing his arms around Clyde's waist and trying to drag him back toward the school. I called after Belton, saying he could walk with me to school. Finally his ma had to pick him up kicking and screaming, since the opening to the mine warn't a safe place for Belton to wander about.

Later on when Miss Clark dismissed us, I saw Belton, pale and distraught, weaving between trees, waiting for Clyde to come out of the schoolhouse.

"Come on, Belton," I said. "I'll take you to your brother. He's up at the mine. I'm goin' there now, so come on . . ." But he wouldn't have it. He ran away from me, going back to his wandering, till he met up with Clyde on his own, I guess.

In general, school was awful lonely without Clyde. Whatever interest I had in my studies was gone. My mind wandered between lessons, and sometimes I felt I'd die if I had to go on listening to kids recite and the teacher lecture hour after hour. My only joy came at recess when the younger kids surrounded me, begging for stories about Walter Barnes and his pack of thieves.

"My old pal Rufus Twilly just wrote me sayin' how Walter and his gangs have built a whole set of tree-houses joined by footbridges that's suspended in midair. They're fixed from one set of branches to another by ropes and special knots that only pirates and other types of rapscallions know to make. This is where they hold folks for ransom, folks they've kidnapped at night by stealin' into open windows and snatchin' 'em from their beds. Oh, my pal Rufus is in terrible danger, for if he tells a livin' soul Walter Barnes is sure to cut his throat. But then again, if the gang's found out, he's off to the chaingang with the lot of 'em, maybe even the firin' squad, for kidnappin's a capital offense."

Seeing their eyes widen with terror was a thousand times more fun than any geography or history lesson ever could be. All day my mind drifted in and out of the lessons. I nodded at Miss Clark like I was paying attention, but all the while I was thinking about my next story, daring myself to spin an even more fantastic yarn about Walter Barnes.

CHAPTER FIFTEEN

A Figure from
My Past
Pays a Visit
and
I Learn More About
My Mysterious Beginnings

"Take it easy, Billy! You're rocking too much in your seat and unsettling Coppers. You can't be doing that in the mines, lad."

I tried to settle myself on the edge of the wagon, but it was awful uncomfortable. The road was rutted and muddy, and my seat bones bounced up and down on the wood. Uncle Jim wouldn't put the seat on for me, because a mule driver sits on the edge of the car.

"You've got to get used to it, rough as it is."

We was finally going to repair Copper's stall and the henhouse. We picked up a load of lumber and feed from the store and was riding through town. Now that I was eleven, I had to spend more time working with Coppers so I could get a job as a mule skinner in the mine. Uncle Jim had me fit in a drive with Coppers whenever we had the time. He sat in the back, wedged between two flour sacks to keep himself steady.

It was payday in Holly Glen, and even though it warn't dark, there was already a few men drunk and staggering through town. The door to the saloon was wide open with miners going in and out. All of 'em was still black with dust. One called to my uncle, beckoning him to join him at the bar.

"Well, if it isn't the bloody Prince of Wales in his royal carriage! Get in here, James Berry, and have us a pint."

Uncle Jim tipped his hat to him. "Carry on without me, Roland. I'm with my nephew. Can't stop."

"Leave the boy! Let him wait outside for the two of us while we have us a few drinks."

"Sorry, Roland, got to get him ready for the mine."

This time the man grumbled back in Welsh, but Uncle Jim just waved back without saying another word. After we got past the saloon, he thanked me.

"What for?" I asked.

"For the excuse, lad, for the excuse. Soon enough he'd be wanting to fight, for Roland's a dreadful drunk. Always looking for a reason to raise his fists after he's had a few."

A mile out of town the woods was thick. We followed the road along the tracks a bit more, then turned back toward home. There warn't a shack or cabin or soul to be seen, so it surprised us when a voice called out.

"You folks going to Holly Glen? C'mon now! Give an old woman a ride."

Uncle Jim and I looked in the voice's direction, scanning the trees until we saw a little old woman walking along the tracks. She was hunched over a cane with a bindle on her back. Her hair was long and white, and I thought for sure she was some kind of witch, but Uncle Jim said no. It was Neva Shyrock, a healer like Aunt Agnes.

"She's the woman who told us about you," said Uncle Jim. "She's coming from Coalgrove. Birthing a baby or nursing a family with fever, no doubt."

"Whoa!" I yelled to Coppers. Uncle Jim jumped out to greet her. He took his hat off and walked up the road. They was happy to see each other, though I couldn't hear the particulars of what they said. Uncle Jim took her bag, and she waddled over to me.

"Billy Creekmore!" she said, staring me straight in the face. "Billy Creekmore! Do you remember me?"

"No, ma'am," I said.

The wind blew her white hair off her face, and I could see she had hardly any teeth left. Her smile was mostly gum. I wasn't sure I liked her knowing who I was.

"I'm the midwife that brought you into this world!"

"I'm awful sorry," I said, "but I don't remember any grown-ups before Peggy and the Beadles."

"That's no matter, no matter at all. But just the same, I'm who borned and raised you your first three years of life. Then I brought you to my cousin, Mrs. Beadle, so she could take you in at the Guardian Angels

Home for Boys. Oh, it's good to see you, Billy Creekmore."

Uncle Jim put her bindle in the back of the wagon, then helped her up, all the while saying how glad Aunt Agnes would be to see her. The two of 'em chattered away, and I heard her say she had another day's walk before she was home. Uncle Jim invited her to spend the night with us so she could get a proper rest, and she thanked him, saying she didn't mind if she did. Her old bones needed it.

Well, I didn't like this at all. It was like having a person who knew all my secrets coming into my new life. I hoped they wouldn't stay up late talking about the strange talent I showed at my birth and how it killed my ma and made my pa run off. I figured I'd have to give up my bed to her and sleep in the corner. Besides that, Neva Shyrock seemed near crazy, and I couldn't tell what type of person she was. Maybe she'd get it in her mind to take me back to her cousin so they could send me to the glassworks and collect a fee from Mr. Colder. Their laughs and chatter made me awful irritable, and I fretted all the way to Holly Glen.

By the time we got home, a full moon was rising. Uncle Jim and I each gave Neva Shyrock an arm to lean on as she stepped out of the wagon. She stopped midway, just before climbing the steps to our cabin, and looked up at the sky.

"Do you hear that, Billy? It's one of the miners floating by, feeling lonesome for his family. Oh, some spirits are awful sad."

She shook her head with sadness, and my blood ran cold watching her. I figured she was sensing the ghost of Clyde's daddy, the same spirit I felt at his gravesite.

"That's right, Billy. I have the gift, same as you, only I had to cultivate mine. Wasn't born to it like you. Oh, I remember it clear, I do—how you'd wave your hands about and talk to the air. Spirits came to you regular from the time you was born."

"I don't remember any of that," I said.

"You don't remember lots of things." She laughed back. "But then, you're too young. You don't realize your memories yet."

I glanced over at Uncle Jim, for I was right uneasy and didn't know what else to say. He seemed ill at ease himself. He cleared his throat a few times, then he called to Aunt Agnes, telling her to come see the surprise waiting for her outside.

The three of 'em sat at the dinner table long into the night. They talked about folks they used to know, which ones had new babies and which ones had died. I was curled up in the corner, trying to cushion myself with blankets, trying my best to fall asleep. Finally they turned in for the night, and Neva Shyrock tucked herself in on my straw mattress by the stove. She coughed and yawned for a while, then started snoring.

Sometime near dawn, I woke with a start, the way you do when you're sleeping someplace new. I guess the same thing had happened to Neva Shyrock, for she was up herself, watching the last of the fire with the covers pulled to her chin.

"Why's your gift so weak? Don't you practice it?" she asked.

I was silent at first, 'cause I warn't sure how much to admit to her. But then I figured she knew the worst about me, so I said, "I just started to. I was afraid to before. Folks said it's what killed my ma and made my father run off and leave me."

"Who told you that?"

"Mrs. Beadle."

Neva Shyrock grumbled. "My cousin's right hysterical. Gets things twisted in her mind 'cause she's so fearful of life. No, Billy, your mother died of fever. She was sick with it before she went into labor. That's what killed her, not you."

"So why'd my pa run off after I was born?"

"He didn't," she said. "He paid me to take care of you and do his laundry while he worked at the ironworks. He came every Sunday to pick up his clothes and give you a bottle. Even took you into Hanging Rock to get you baptized. He got tired of the ironworks, though, so he took off looking for other work."

I was wide awake now, listening to every word. "Did you ever see him again?"

"He came back two years later to see you and give me a couple dollars. He took you down by the creek to throw some stones in the water and said you was a fine-looking boy, full of energy and health. He thanked me for looking after you so good, then he 'pologized for not giving me more money than he did. He was heading out the door, but I told him I couldn't sit still no more waiting for his money to arrive. I had to get back to traveling about and healing folks, so I could make a living myself. That's when I told him 'bout my cousin's orphanage. Fair enough, he said, just give him the address, for one day he'd come get you."

"He said he'd come for me?" I asked.

"Yes, he did."

It made me tremulous to hear it, though I couldn't quite say if I was happy or sad. Why, my father never really abandoned me. He done his best to care for me, and one day he'd be coming to get me!

"Did he say when he'd come get me?"

"No, he didn't. Your pa warn't one for details." Then she started yawning and talking slower and slower till finally she fell back asleep.

I listened to her snoring and sputtering, all the while figuring how my father would come get me. I reckoned he'd show up at the orphanage first. Maybe Mr. Beadle would tell him where I was or maybe he wouldn't. In any case, I felt sure Peggy or Rufus would take him aside and tell him I was here in Holly Glen. And then, when he showed up here, what would I say to Uncle Jim and Aunt Agnes? I felt a pang of guilt, knowing how sad they'd be when I left. I hoped they wouldn't think I was ungrateful for all they had done for me. In the end, I figured, they'd understand. After all, a boy should be with his father.

When I woke for school the next day, Neva Shyrock was still sleeping, and when I got home that afternoon, she was long gone. My heart sank. Listening to Neva's memories made my parents a little less shadowy, and a little more real. I was hoping to hear more stories, to get a better picture of them in my mind, but it warn't to be. My tin box of cards and a necklace was still the closest thing to them I had. Aunt Agnes said she tried to give Neva some money to take the train, but she insisted on walking. The spring air would do her good, she said. She took the money, though, saying she'd use it to buy some new bottles for her remedies.

CHAPTER SIXTEEN

I'M WARNED TO KEEP QUIET *ABOUT CERTAIN THINGS* *and* RECEIVE TROUBLING NEWS *FROM RUFUS*

Before long, school was out and days was long and almost lazy. After chores, I went fishing or for a swim. I always took my slingshot for a little target practice. Mostly I'd shoot at a dead branch or an old beehive if I saw one. Boys in Holly Glen were good shots, and lots of families ate squirrel and pigeon regular, but I didn't care for hunting of any kind. Some boys was told to go out and hunt for dinner, but Aunt Agnes and Uncle Jim warn't that way. After I had pumped the day's water, fed the chickens, and milked Trotwood, they let me wander the woods or swim as I pleased. I was getting good with my whip, and could knock over cans galore and just about put out the flame of a candle, though I was still knocking it over more times than I left it standing.

Days passed by pleasant enough, but in general, I was bored and stifled since Clyde was down in the mine and I didn't have a friend my age to play with. Just like at school, I was stuck with the little kids tagging about. They followed me to the swimming hole and through the woods and hung about my yard, asking for stories about Walter Barnes.

"Oh, he was a mean one," I said as I cracked my whip. "He sold a little chap by the name of Milas Kincaid to the gypsies for a twenty-dollar gold piece and all the wine he could drink. He'd sneak out at night and go visit them at their camp, which was just down-river from the orphanage. He'd dance to their violins and drink up a storm. He promised to steal more boys, which they roasted and ate . . ."

"He sounds like the Devil himself! What else did he do?" said little Frank Moon. He was near eight and awful impressionable. He'd sit on the fence watching me practice tricks with my whip and beg for another chapter. Each time my whip cracked he jumped, but no matter how scared he got, he wouldn't let me alone and always came back to hear more about Walter Barnes. His daddy, John Moon, was Welsh, and he came over regular for visits with Uncle Jim. Sooner or later, the two of 'em would lapse into Welsh, which is an altogether different language, and Aunt Agnes and I couldn't understand a thing they said.

"You . . . Billy Creekmore. Come out here . . . ," John Moon said to me one summer evening. He and Uncle Jim was on the porch in our two rocking chairs, smoking their pipes and taking in the cool air. "What are these stories you're telling my boy? And will you stop it now, for the lad can't sleep for fear of Walter Barnes, whoever he is, stealing him from his bed at night. . . ."

"Telling stories, is he? What's all this about, Billy?" Aunt Agnes had come out on the porch to hear my response. She tossed her dishcloth over her shoulder and put her hands on her hips.

"Well, uh, Mr. Moon . . . sometimes . . . when they ask me, that is . . . I tell the younger ones stories about the orphanage I was at."

"What kind of stories?" asked Aunt Agnes. She wasn't at all happy to hear this, and she looked at me with a cold face.

"Oh, you know . . . stories about the boys I knew . . . funny stories . . ."

"I haven't heard about any funny stories, only scary ones, mostly about an evil boy named Walter Barnes who robs and steals and sells children to the gypsies. Frank's just a wee lad, Billy. Will you stop it, please? I can't sleep at night for his crying."

"No more stories, Billy," said Uncle Jim. "A miner's work is too dangerous to go about it half dead with fatigue."

Aunt Agnes shook her head in disgust. "Don't worry none, John. He'll stop his tales about Walter Barnes, won't you, Billy? There'll be trouble if you don't." She gave me a stern look, then stomped off to the kitchen.

"Don't be harsh on him, Agnes," Mr. Moon called after her. "He didn't mean any harm by it. I'd wager he's bored, wishing to be with his friend Clyde and the older boys in the mine. How old is he now, Jim? He'll be down with us soon enough, won't he?"

"He'll be there before long. Has his mind set on being a mule driver, he does."

"You could start him now if you want," said Mr. Moon. "I've seen him with Coppers and the wagon. He did a fine job keeping him steady when you picked up that load of lumber. He's good enough to learn the trade."

"Oh yes, Uncle Jim, please let me . . . I'm the oldest boy in school and I don't want to go back come September."

"We'll see, lad, we'll see . . . I'll talk to the foreman soon enough to see if there's an opening for you. You'll be there before you know it. Don't be rushing to go into the mines, lad."

"That's right, Billy." Mr. Moon nodded. "Listen to your uncle now. It's a hard life, isn't it, Jim?"

"Yes, it is, John, but it pays better here than in Wales."

"That it does, but I'm awful tired of the company's cheating ways. It's the cribbing I hate most of all. That and the prices at the company store. Did you know they raised the price of blasting powder again? And picks as well. And if we buy our equipment in Charleston where it's cheaper, we get fired!"

"What's cribbin'?" I asked the men. I knew all about the company store, and was bitter over its high prices like everyone else in town. But I hadn't heard the word "cribbing" before.

"Cribbing is how Mr. Newgate squeezes a bit more blood and money out of us miners, lad," said Mr. Moon. "Last year he added a frame round the top of his coal cars so they hold four tons now instead of three. But does he pay us any more per car? No, lad, he pays us the same, as if we were only loading three tons a car instead of four."

"But that's cheatin'!" I said.

"Of course it is, lad, but Mr. Newgate calls it fair. He says we was filling the cars with slate and rubble when he's paying for coal. I'm telling you, Jim, a union would help us! We need the United Mine Workers here in Holly Glen."

"Now, John, be careful. Didn't Mr. Newgate say he'd send in the guards from the Baldwin-Felts Agency to evict any miner who supports the union?"

"A miner was evicted down the road just a few years ago. A terrible thing it was," piped in Aunt Agnes. She joined the men on the porch, angry as I'd ever seen her. "Kicking a family out of their home in the middle of winter!"

"That's why we need the union!" said Mr. Moon.

"That's why we have to be quiet, John. And watch what we say and who we say it to," said Uncle Jim. "We need to see what happens in the other mining towns along Paint Creek. I want to know how much the union is willing to help us before we start demanding things from Mr. Newgate."

Aunt Agnes cut him off. "Mind how you talk in front of Billy, you two. He'll be working in the mine before long. Now, Billy, you forget all about this. Not a shred of your storytelling nonsense about what you just heard. Don't say the word union to a living soul, and if folks ever try talking to you about it, act like you don't know what they mean. Do you hear me?"

"Yes, ma'am," I said. And I meant it, too. I could tell the union was a dangerous thing to discuss.

"Good. Now get in the kitchen and help me with the last of the washing."

It was Friday, and Mr. Moon and my uncle talked long into the night. They started speaking in Welsh, so I don't know if they talked more about the union or Mr. Newgate. Whatever they were saying, it was a passionate discussion. Mr. Moon slapped his hand on the arm of his chair more than once, and Uncle Jim smoked pipe after pipe while he rocked in his chair.

For the time being, it was easy to forget what I heard about the union and the Baldwin-Felts guards, 'cause I had plenty to think about. Neva Shyrock had told me the truth about the night I was born. Then, there were two other things occupying my mind. One was hearing Uncle Jim say he'd be talking to the foreman soon and that finally I'd be getting a job in the mine. The other was a letter from Rufus that set me to worrying so bad, I couldn't sleep at night. Seems he'd taken to spying at night whenever he heard that Mr. Colder was coming to dine. Just like I did, he'd sneak out in the dark and hide under the dining room window.

> *You can imagine how scared I got hearing Mr. Beadle offering me to Mr. Colder to apprentice in his factory. Peggy heard it too when she was clearing their plates after supper, and we spoke about it the next day. She says the same thing you did—that it's no type of life for a boy. She's putting money and food aside and helping me plan how to run away to Albright, where I can hide out for a while until I figure out where to go next. So, Billy, this might be the last letter you get from me for a long time.*

Well, I got right quivery reading this letter and thinking about Rufus stealing away and hiding about in the night. It was over a year since I last saw him, but even so I couldn't imagine him being big enough to either work in the glassworks or take off on his own. Where'd he sleep at night? What would he do once the food ran out? I suppose he could always sneak back to the orphanage for a handout from Peggy. I knew she'd be good for it, but how Rufus could manage on his own I couldn't begin to figure. I thought about the Cheat River and how it took Meek. I wished there was some way Rufus could come here and make a home with Aunt Agnes, Uncle Jim, and me here in Holly Glen, but it was already too late to send word to him. He might be out in the dark wandering the very moment I read his letter.

I fretted over Rufus for days until I figured there was nothing I could do except hope for his safety. I went back to practicing my whip, and finally, one day I managed to put out a flame and leave the candle still standing. It was early evening and the sun was still out. I called Aunt Agnes and Uncle Jim.

"Look! I can do it now!" I lit the candle and stepped back from it about ten feet. I brought my arm back and snapped the whip. *Crack!* The very fringes of the tip brushed the flame and put it out just like that. A thin ribbon of blue smoke curled upward. I puffed up with pride. Aunt Agnes and Uncle Jim clapped for me.

"There you go, lad! Congratulations! You're ready to meet the foreman," said Uncle Jim. "I'll take you to the mine with me tomorrow to see if he has a job for you. Now it's time to learn about your safety lamp. I bought one for you not long ago, and I best show you how to light it before your first day."

The next morning I was awake before the mine whistle. I slung my whip over my shoulder, and Uncle Jim helped me hook my lamp on my cap.

"Here you go," said Aunt Agnes, handing me my lunch pail. "I baked you a cherry pie." She looked me in the eye for a moment, and I could tell she wanted to tell me to be careful, only it warn't her manner to do so.

We left the house, and she walked with us for a while, then hung back to talk with some of the other women. Clyde Light spied me and came tearing over.

"Good to see ya!" he said. "I was wondering when you'd finally get here!"

The sun was coming up as we tramped up the mountain. Some of the spraggers gave me a hard look and a smirk, and Clyde told 'em to steer off and keep to themselves.

"This here's Billy Creekmore," he said, "and he's going straight to being a mule driver."

"Sure he is," sneered one of 'em. "I'll be seeing you inside, Billy Creekmore!"

"Don't mind him. He's scared of the rats. Hates seeing 'em run through the mines. One of the boys tied a dead one to his lunch pail by its tail and scared him half to death."

"You don't say. A big guy like that afraid of rats . . . ," I said back. I couldn't admit that I hated rats myself. I hoped there warn't near as many rats running through the mine as I heard folks say.

The foreman was at the entrance of the mine, checking in the miners, giving them their id tags for the coal cars they'd fill, and waving hello. He was a secret looking man, with one side of his face twisted up.

"Mr. Wheeton, this here's my nephew Billy Creekmore. He's ready to work in the mine now. Wants to be a mule skinner."

"Most boys start out as trappers or spraggers in the mine." One of his eyes half shut, like he was taking aim at something with an invisible gun. He looked at me like I was a target, and I could tell he didn't like anything too out of the ordinary on his watch.

"Yes, sir, it was that way in Wales, too. But Billy's talented with a whip, and he's been working old Coppers for quite a while now. He's a clever boy, too, can learn a trade quick as any his age or older."

Things didn't seem to be going my way, so I decided to pipe in. "Why, Mr. Wheeton, when I was only ten I was all set to work in the glassworks since I was known far and wide to be such a fast learner. Mr. Colder was gonna assign me straightaway to the main furnace, but along come my uncle to have me live here in Holly Glen."

Uncle Jim gave me a glance, but it seemed I did some good.

"Well," said the foreman, "we can always use a good skinner. . . . I'll give him a try." Then he whistled over another mule skinner the name of Clayton Nicewander and told him I'd be following him about for the day.

"Oh, will he, Mr. Wheeton? And will you be paying me extra for teaching the boy his trade? I'm sure I'll do it to your specifications, sir." He gave Mr. Wheeton a little bow, and then spit some tobacco near his boots.

Mr. Wheeton jumped back, but a little bit of tobacco juice hit his toe. He fixed on Clayton with his one open eye, all bright with meanness. "No, I won't be paying you extra, just like I didn't pay the boy extra who taught you, Clayton. Now get along. Learn quick, Billy, and, Clayton, don't cause no trouble."

Inside the mine, Clyde and Uncle Jim peeled off one way, and Clayton and I went another toward the stables.

"Good luck!" called Clyde.

"We'll see you at the end of the day," said Uncle Jim.

I had never been inside the mine before. The ceiling was held up with rows and rows of timbers, which is nothing more than tree trunks stripped of bark and branches. The light of my lamp wouldn't let me see more than several feet ahead of me. Beyond that was the deepest kind of darkness I'd ever been in. It was blacker than pitch, all velvety and thick without no light of any kind. It was cold in there, too, and the sides of the tunnels was wet. I could hear water dripping into a pool, but where it was I couldn't tell. Worse than that was the sound of timbers creaking and groaning in the distance.

"Is the mine cavin' in?" I asked Clayton. I was dreadful afraid all of a sudden. The startling sounds and fierce blackness all around me was making me right jumpity.

"It will if they don't put up more timbers. That's coming from the old part of the mine. The roof's settling and squeezing 'em so bad they're splintering from the pressure. I'll take you to see 'em. It's quite a sight. Some look just like bent elbows. That part of the mine is near run out of coal now. The company's pushing the miners to get it out fast before the roof collapses."

"Why don't they put in more timbers?"

"'Cause the coal's almost gone and the company don't wanna spend the money. Besides, the mine boss says there ain't no danger of a cave-in. Says all that creaking and splintering is just the mountain settling and nothing to worry about." Clayton laughed a bit, then took his whip off and cracked it into the dark. "Now don't start getting the cold shivers, Billy. You've only just begun."

CHAPTER SEVENTEEN

An Account of My First Days in the Mine *as Well as of* the Circus That Came to Charleston

Clayton Nicewander was rude to Mr. Wheeton and didn't take no nonsense from the spraggers, but he was a good teacher. He was sixteen years old, five years older than me, and as patient as I needed. He didn't laugh or yell when I fumbled with my lamp or forgot which part of the mine to visit first. He taught me everything I needed to know, from how to get the stubbornest mule to work a bit longer to how to find my way to safety if my lamp fell or burned out and I was stranded in the dark.

"The mule knows the way, even in the pitch dark without no light at all. Just get off the car, feel your way to her side and take off her harness. Throw an arm over her back and walk with her toward the stable. She'll lead you to one of the miners or back to the stable, and you can hold on just like that all the way there. A man loses all sense of direction in total darkness, but that don't happen to a mule. So you've got to rely on her to get to safety."

Some of the mules was more stubborn than others, and one day when we was driving an old fellow named Piston, I cracked my whip on his backside and kicked him in his rear to get him going.

"Don't be doing that!" scolded Clayton. "He ain't even carrying half a car. If you have to whip him now, you'll never get him to carry four cars of coal for you!"

"Well, how do I get him to move, then?"

"You gotta make him think you're gonna whip him. Crack a warning in the air 'bout three feet above his ears. If he still won't move, crack it again, only lower.

Then again if you have to, but don't do more than sting the tips of his ears. Otherwise he'll get used to being whipped. Then he'll figure out that it ain't as bad as hauling eight tons of coal and you're sunk. He'll lie down on the tracks and won't move at all, letting you whip him all you please. But he won't pull any coal for you. Then he'll send word around to the other mules that you're a cruel driver, and none of 'em will work for you. I ain't figured out how they communicate like that, but they do."

Clayton taught me all the different routes in the mine. He told me which ones to visit first and how to keep pace with the miners.

"Don't take off till you double-check the miner slipped his tag on the car. See here?" He pointed to a curved nail at the front of the car. "Each miner has his own number engraved on a brass tag. He puts it right here on this hook. If it's not there, the foreman won't credit him for all that coal he loaded and he's out his money."

Some miners was angry every time they saw us, complaining we was lazy and slow and making 'em lose money. Others said nothing, just gave us a quick nod when we coupled their full car and left an empty one behind. I was glad to see Uncle Jim on our route.

"How you doing there, Billy? How you doing, Clayton?" he asked. He stopped digging at the face to chat, asking how things were going in one part of the mine or how Clayton's mother was getting on. She was a widow, and just like Clyde's ma she ran one of the company boardinghouses. Clayton's pa and older brother died when he was just three. They was suffocated by the black damp, which is a type of poison gas that builds up when the coal is pulled out of the earth.

Clayton said not to worry none about the angry fellows. He said it warn't nothing personal, just what happens to some men because of the nature of the work.

"A miner only gets paid for the coal he produces. But before he can fill up a car, there's a whole lot of things he has to do that he ain't paid for." He went on to tell me how the miner's got to chip away at the bottom of the face, then blast into it with explosives, then dig out the rubble to get to a new seam of coal in the mountain. The company gives 'em the timbers to support the roof, but the miner has to put 'em in place. Likewise, the company provides the track, but the miner has to lay it into the room. "All this takes two days or more, and he ain't paid for any of it. A miner don't earn a dime till he fills that car we bring 'em with coal, and then he only gets twenty cents a ton. Much as I don't like being yelled at, I understand the angry miners. Miners get a raw deal from the company."

Once he finished training me, Clayton would be driving a two-mule team and getting a man's wages. I was glad to know I'd be seeing him regular, though. He'd be at the stables in the morning when we was picking up our mules and at the end of the workday when we was feeding 'em and cleaning out their stables. On our last day working together, he introduced me to my mule, Markel.

"Markel's a decent mule," he said, scratching him between the ears. "He was my mule when I first came to the mine. Remember to whip just above his ears and not his backside and he'll work hard for ya."

"How old is he?" I asked. I took over scratching him and looked into his huge eyes. They was shiny and dark.

"Can't say. He was here before I come, probably spent all but a few weeks of his life in the mine."

"Imagine. A whole life in the mine."

"Don't say it, Billy." Clayton groaned. "I don't wish that on any creature."

That evening we came out of the mine to see the whole town had been papered with circus posters. There must have been a hundred of 'em, plastered on every fence and building and lightpost from Main Street to the depot. My eyes ricocheted from one to the other as I walked home. Over and over we read the same thing, that for one night only in Charleston . . .

The Frederick Ainsworth Circus

Presents

KING SOLOMON AND THE QUEEN OF SHEBA:

AN EXOTIC SPECTACLE OF ANCIENT DAYS

Uncle Jim was as thrilled as anyone to see the posters. He nearly dropped his pick and lunch pail in the streets with happiness, and, just like he said he would, he took me to see the circus. He invited Clyde and Belton to come with us, but only Clyde came since Belton was too excitable for a circus. Aunt Agnes had "no interest whatsoever in such foolishness." She told us to watch for the pickpockets that worked the crowds and said she'd just as soon stay home and get some work done. "I'll spend the day boiling my herbs and making tinctures for the coming winter."

Uncle Jim loved the parade as much as the show, so we left Holly Glen on an early train and got into Charleston by noon. We walked from the station into town till we got to the courthouse, where Uncle Jim said we'd have a good view of the parade. Plenty of Charleston folks had already staked out their places, but I couldn't complain none. We had a fine view when the parade came by a few hours later.

In the meantime, we ate our lunch on the steps. Afterward Uncle Jim let Clyde and me wander through town while he saved our seats. Oh, Charleston's a beautiful town, with paved sidewalks and fine buildings. Seemed like every wooden one was painted a nice color. Others were made of brick or granite, and some was even carved from solid marble. The marble ones was mostly banks. They had gold grates over the windows, all fancied and filigreed, but strong, too, so a robber couldn't bust through and take the money. Uncle Jim gave us each a nickel to get an ice cream. I asked if he wanted us to bring him back a cone, but he said no, he didn't want none. Just sitting in the shade resting his eyes was all the treat he needed.

Finally, the parade begun and all the folks sitting on the steps stood up to whoop and clap and wave their hats. First came the most magnificent white and gold carriage led by eight white horses with red plumes on their heads. Up top was a swarm of ladies waving at us. They was dressed like temple dancers, with flowing veils and fans of peacock feathers, and gold bracelets round their arms. All the circus folk was dressed from the time of Egypt, which pleased Uncle Jim to no end since he was right fond of old-time things. The last circus he saw was called "King Arthur and His Merry Knights," and he was delighted this one was so different.

"Look at that, boys!" he said when the tumblers came by, dressed in gold pantaloons and doing their flips and twists easy as pie right there in the street."Oh, the glory of it! Oh, if only my mother were alive to see it. How she loved the tumblers!"

Some desert Arabs on their stallions was next, looking as lofty and airy as you please. Then came some more gorgeous wagons, all painted right pretty and gaudy, carrying the fiercest tigers and lions, each one growling away and swiping between the bars. Another pack of ladies in temple costumes came next, dancing about with bells round their ankles, playing little cymbals and kicking up their legs. In and out of the whole throng of performers was a pair of clowns chasing each other. Their faces was painted white and they wore the tiniest little hats and played the most bent up out-of-tune instruments you ever did hear. Clyde and I laughed our heads off at 'em for they was so quick and rambunctious. They kicked one of the tumblers in the pants, then ran off before he could catch 'em, interrupting the jugglers and making 'em drop their balls, and so forth.

We followed the tail end of the parade to the circus grounds. Hundreds of folks was there for the show. Kids ran about laughing and calling out, begging their parents for an extra penny to buy some cotton candy or a candied apple. Uncle Jim bought us a program to read while we waited for the show to begin. On the back page was a list of all the cities the circus would tour. One wasn't far from Albright, and I wished that somehow or other my old friends Peggy and Rufus could see it.

For a little while, even while the band was playing and the ringmaster led out one of the clowns with his pack of trick dogs, I felt lonesome for them. I couldn't enjoy what was in front of me for wondering what fate had befallen Rufus, and wishing that somehow he and Peggy might be able to see the spectacle Clyde, Uncle Jim, and I was about to enjoy.

For a while I was right sad, but I have to say I was taken over by what was before me, for the circus was splendid, even better than the parade. The dancing and dramatic parts told the story of how the Queen of Sheba sailed along the Nile with all her dancing girls and slaves to seek counsel from King Solomon. He greeted her with all manner of beasts, including camels and lions, as well as musicians and dancers of his own.

Then he gave her a great party with jugglers and acrobats for entertainment. Later on, she tried tricking him with fake flowers to see how wise he really was. When he passed her test, she poured out all her troubles and implored him to help her. He set her straight on all that ailed her, and back to Sheba she went in her radiant barge, with Solomon and all his folks waving good-bye.

In between scenes from the story were all kinds of acts. There was fire-eaters, animal tamers, trapeze artists, tightrope walkers, and even a wild west show where the horseman acted out Custer's defeat at Little Big Horn, including the part where Custer gets scalped. It was so realistic Clyde and I hid our eyes. Otherwise, I was right transfixed, couldn't take my eyes off 'em for the Indians was stunning trick riders. I decided right then and there that's what I'd want to be if I was ever lucky enough to be in a circus. One stood on the back of his galloping stallion to throw a tomahawk at General Custer, and he was calm and steady like he was standing on a chair. Uncle Jim out and out booed it, saying a wild west scene had no part in a spectacle 'bout King Solomon and the Queen of Sheba.

Despite this, Uncle Jim agreed with me and Clyde that it was a right bully circus, the splendidest one that could ever be. We walked back through town to the train station, laughing and arguing about which was the best part. Clyde and I fell asleep in the waiting room till the train arrived sometime past midnight. Uncle Jim helped us get on board and find some seats, and then we fell back asleep until we arrived home in Holly Glen. We walked Clyde to his house, then stumbled into ours, sleeping sound till late Sunday morning.

When we woke, Aunt Agnes had a big breakfast for us. She sat with us as we ate and wanted to hear all about the show. Much as she liked our recounting of it, she was glad she didn't go. She'd prepared all her remedies and was ready for winter. It was going to be a nasty year for the grippe. She could tell by the way the leaves were drying up so soon without turning orange.

CHAPTER EIGHTEEN

I Daydream Too Much,
and Learn About
THE UMW,
RATS,
and
a Ghost

Oh, but I thought about the circus plenty while I was deep in the mine. There I'd be, driving Markel, and I'd see myself as one of the trick riders making his stallion race around lightning quick with its mane all ripply in the wind. Sometimes I saw Markel and me thundering across the plains all set to attack General Custer. I liked that part of the circus, even though Uncle Jim found fault with it.

"Are you my stallion, Markel?" I'd say as I fed him lumps of sugar, which is what Clayton said I should do if I wanted him to work hard for me. "Do you want me to braid your mane with little bows and get you a spangled headdress?" Markel loved sandwiches and pie, but wasn't too keen on the cold potato Aunt Agnes packed in the lower tray of my pail. Neither was I, to be honest, but you don't mind bland food when you're hungry.

Plenty of miners got awful angry at me 'cause I was stuck in daydreams and not keeping up with 'em. I couldn't remember who was spending the morning undercutting and who was filling up a car. All I could think about was the trick riders, and how one of 'em was blindfolded but managed to somersault from one galloping horse to another. Oh, it was a grand thing to see! And awful thrilling since you didn't know how he could possibly know where the next horse was and if he missed he'd break his neck and get trampled. How I wanted to be a daring horseman, riding around with an audience cheering me on! But the roof of the mine was too low for me to stand on Markel's back. And then, of course, I didn't have no time at all to waste learning any kind of trick down there. I'd show up at the wrong room at the wrong time, and the miner was getting ready to drill a bit of blasting powder into the face.

"What you doing here, Billy? You know I've been undercutting all morning. I won't have a car of coal for another two hours!" Then down the corridor I'd hear a miner yelling my name, "Creekmore! Billy Creekmore, git over here! You're costing me money, boy!" A good miner shoveled ten tons of coal a day, and he sure didn't want me standing in his way.

Lots of the miners was angry men, just like Clayton said, and I overheard more and more of 'em talking about the United Mine Workers when I passed by on my route. Every now and then, one of 'em would say something to me about how the UMW needed young boys like me to stand with 'em. Fortunately I remembered what Aunt Agnes said, and the words spilled outta me easy enough.

"Boys like you should join the union," said one miner to me. "After all, you've got more to gain than an old man like me. You've got a lifetime in the mine ahead of you, and the union can help you."

"Oh, but I already belong to the union at church," I said. "I go there every Sunday and every other weeknight for union with God and my fellow man."

"Well, the union I'm talking about is different," he went on. "It's more about standing up for your rights and not letting Mr. Newgate run your life to make himself rich."

"Oh, yes, I pray regular for Mr. Newgate and for all of us down here workin' in the dangers. . . . Well, I best be off. Giddap, Markel!" I cracked my whip in the air and hurried away into the blackness.

Day after day, deep in the mine, I felt some of the old loneliness that used to cling to me at the orphanage. I figured it was the darkness of the mine coupled with the solitude of my job. Three times a day, I pulled a load of coal from the farthest part of the mine way up to the weighing station, and I'd be alone in the dark for long stretches of time. The yellow light from my lamp cast weak shadows on the damp walls. As the clop-clop of the mule echoed in the tunnels, I'd get to thinking about things—like the way Mr. Beadle beat Herbert Mullens so bad he stopped talking or how fearful Meek Jones looked after he drowned.

Plenty of folks believed the mines was haunted by all the miners that died there, and sometimes I felt something following me and Markel. It was awful unsettling. The hairs on the back of my neck stood up, and I'd turn around quick to look behind me.

"Who's there?"

My voice echoed down the dark passageways till it was swallowed up in black. Nothing answered back.

"I bet you was feeling the ghost of little Golden Breedlove," said Clyde. "He was a trapper like me, about ten years old. A coal car run off its tracks and crushed him against the wall of the mine."

Clyde was working the trap near the old part of the mine, sitting on his little bench eating lunch. I strapped a bag of oats to Markel, and sat next to Clyde with my sandwich.

"How long ago was that?"

"Oh, I'd say it was ten years ago . . . back when the mine first opened. He was the first boy kilt in the mine. Folks say his spirit wanders about trying to find its way out to the light."

"I felt like somethin' was followin' me . . . But it warn't a mean ghost. It was a sad ghost that wanted me to take it somewhere."

"That would be Golden, I reckon. He was thinking you'd lead him outta the mine. Folks say his mother went crazy with grief. Morning, noon, and night she wandered about the mine entrance looking for him. Then one day she was found drowned in Paint Creek. She filled up her pockets with stones and walked into the water."

A swarm of rats, twenty or more, and big as kittens, scurried under the trapper door, then under our bench. A fat one, bold as can be, came out to face us and stood up on its hind legs like a squirrel, begging for food. "This is my pal Jo-Jo. He's so fat 'cause I feed him." Clyde tore off a piece of his sandwich and threw it to him.

"Aaagh! How can you stand 'em?" I moaned. "I hate their bald tails and fat bellies."

"Don't you know the rats are a miner's best friend? They'll let you know if a roof's about to collapse or if the gases are collecting. Their ears are better than ours and their whiskers feel the tiniest vibration. They sense rock grinding and hear timbers splintering long before we do."

"Oh, I hate 'em!" I said. "They swarm about Markel's stall, eatin' his feed and nestin' in his straw."

"That may be," said Clyde, "but if you ever see a pack of 'em running somewhere, you better drop what you're doing and run with 'em. Besides that, they keep me company. I get so lonely here hour after hour, I've turned 'em into my pets, especially Jo-Jo."

I could hardly bear watching 'em squirm over each other, fighting for food. They was bothering me too much to eat peacefully, so Clyde said to go ahead and crack my whip to scare 'em off. Clyde warn't bothered none. He said Jo-Jo and his friends would be back.

CHAPTER NINETEEN

Mr. Newgate's Practices

GIVE ME A DESIRE

TO LEARN POLISH,

but

DISASTER STRIKES

BEFORE I CAN

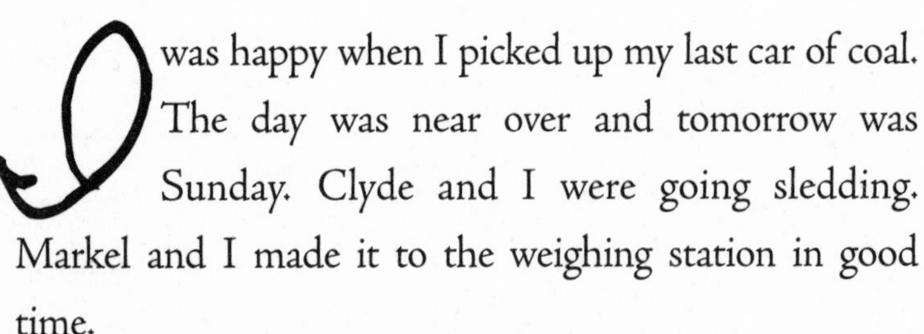

I was happy when I picked up my last car of coal. The day was near over and tomorrow was Sunday. Clyde and I were going sledding. Markel and I made it to the weighing station in good time.

"You're doing better," said Clayton. He was already there, of course, checking over his deliveries with the supervisor. "The miners aren't gonna yell at you so much." He slapped his gloves against his leg to get some of the dust off.

Just then, the ceiling above us shook a little. Muffled rumblings sounded deep in the mine.

"What's that?" I asked.

Even the supervisor looked alarmed. He scooted off to the main hallway to take a look.

"That's the ceiling in the old corridor," said Clayton. "It's gonna collapse before long."

The mine boss met up with the supervisor, and the two of 'em was pointing and talking in hushed tones. Clayton watched 'em with an angry look on his face.

"The Poles are working there," he said. "Oh, it's perfect for the company, ain't it? None of 'em speaks enough English to complain."

"I wish I spoke Polish so I could warn 'em," I said. I could see myself whispering to 'em on my route, then tipping my hat to the mine boss on my way out, easy as you please. "Maybe I'll learn."

"I just hope I'm nowhere near when the collapse finally comes," said Clayton. "Until then, I'm watching the rats."

The sledding warn't too good the next day. The snow was old and thin, so it was slow going down the hill. Mostly Clyde and I spent our time roaming through town looking for icicles. They hung from the rafters of different buildings here and there, fierce and angry looking. Some were nearly two feet long. We took turns keeping each other steady as one climbed atop a fence post to wrench 'em free. When each of us had an armful, we walked down to the tracks and threw 'em like spears. Our eyes trailed 'em till we saw a tiny explosion of shattered ice in the distance. When the icicles were gone, we ran up to see what we'd done. About a million pieces of ice were flung around the tracks, all sharp and glittery like broken glass. Some had sunk through the snow, and others had landed right on top of the tracks. I guess they stayed there till the next train came and melted 'em away in an instant.

I threw those icicles so hard that my shoulder was

sore the next day. I couldn't lift the sack of lime to sprinkle over the straw in Markel's stall without groaning.

"What's wrong with you?" asked Clayton.

"I think I threw my arm out. Clyde and I were throwin' icicles all day."

"Well, heck, Billy," he said. "You gotta have more sense. You're a working man now." He took the sack from me and started spreading it around.

Suddenly, a rumbling echoed deep in the mountain, only this time it was so strong that the floor beneath us started rocking. It grew louder and louder till the whole mine was filled with the sound of boulders and rubble crashing against each other.

"Brace yourself, Billy! The old corridor's coming down!" yelled Clayton. But the floor was pitching too hard for me, and I was knocked to the ground. Clayton was next, and he tumbled on top of me, pinning me so hard against the wall that I couldn't breathe for a bit. That's when I started getting panicky, 'cause I couldn't tell if it was him or a mound of rubble burying me.

Somehow he righted himself, then he picked me up

and started yelling at me to get up and keep standing, no matter what.

"Keep your head up, Billy, your shoulders, too, so we can dig our way out if we have to."

Bits of rock and debris flew through the corridor into my eyes and throat, and I started coughing something fierce. Then, just as suddenly as it started, the shaking stopped, and even though we could hear the sound of boulders and timbers crashing elsewhere, our end of the mine was still. Coal dust hung in the air like smoke.

I grabbed Markel's reins and was all set to go, but Clayton made me leave him behind.

"Don't bother, Billy. Mr. Newgate'll buy a new mule, but he won't pay for our funerals. C'mon now. Someone's lamp is likely to ignite all the coal dust in the air and the whole mine will explode."

An alarm whistle pierced the stillness, which struck me as odd and funny in a way, considering that it was after the fact. What we really needed was an alarm that went off before a collapse, but I guess Mr. Newgate hadn't thought of that.

Miners were streaming through the corridor. Some

were panicky and pushing their way to the entrance; others were walking calm as could be with their picks and shovels and lunch pails just like it was quitting time of any other day. A few were bleeding from where a rock or a falling timber had grazed 'em, and one old miner was dragging a crushed foot while two of his buddies helped him out.

Seeing him made me think of Uncle Jim and Clyde, and I ran into the crowd of miners, dodging the ones who were running by me and pushing past the slower ones. All of 'em looked alike, with their blackened clothes and faces, so I searched the crowd for one who was a head shorter than most, and then an even shorter one with blond hair sticking out of his cap.

In a flash, Clayton was after me, yanking me by my collar and yelling.

"You can't go back there!"

I tried squirming out of his grasp, but he was too strong for me.

"I've got to find my uncle and Clyde."

"You can't, Billy! It's too dangerous! C'mon now. They might be out already."

He threw an arm around me and near dragged me back a few steps. More and more folks rushed past us now, and I could hear some men yelling near the entrance to the old section. They called for the fire crew to get in there quick, and I could tell that there was nothing any of us could do unless we was part of a rescue team. So I gave up trying, and ran into daylight with Clayton.

Already the mine boss had ordered the entrance to the mine to be fenced off so that the families of the miners trapped inside wouldn't go crazy with fear and grief and run in to find their kin. The rest of us was pushed away while a crew of men stretched out a length of chain link. Everyone was looking for their family and friends, and the same questions kept being asked over and over. Where were you when it happened? Who else was with you? Did you see old Pete, or any of the Poles? Did anyone in the old corridor make it out, or are all of 'em buried under the rubble?

Seemed like we broke up by nationalities, with the Italian miners at one end, the Welshmen at the other, and the colored and Russian, Romanian and native born in between. None of the Polish miners was there.

After Clayton found his mother, he walked me over to the Welshmen to wait for Uncle Jim. Mr. Moon was there, talking to the others.

"Don't worry about your uncle," said Mr. Moon. "He was working the face farthest from the old corridor. He'll be limping out soon enough."

Little Frank Moon lit up when he saw me. He broke away from his pa to grab hold of my wrist and beg me for a story about Walter Barnes.

"Not now," I told him, but he didn't let up on me till I had to push him away. *What the heck did he think was going on?* I wondered. I kept my eyes on the slow trickle of men coming outta the mine.

Finally, a small man with a stream of blood down the side of his face hobbled out slowly.

It was Uncle Jim!

I ran over to him, and he pulled us close, saying, "Bless you, lad! Bless you, and thank God you're safe."

"What happened to you?" The blood was running bright and red down his pants now.

"Nothing your aunt can't stitch up for me. One of

the rocks flying through caught my forehead. How are you, lad? Where were you when it happened?"

"I was in the stables. Clayton here helped me out."

"Oh, thank you, Clayton, thank you."

He shook Clayton's hand, bloody and all, then he asked, "What about Clyde? Where was he today?"

"He was workin' the trap near the old tunnel," I answered.

Even behind the blood stains and the coal on his face, I could see Uncle Jim's expression fall. A sense of dread fell over me, and I suddenly felt weary, like my bones was collapsing. Somehow, in that second, I knew Clyde was dead.

Uncle Jim must have read my thoughts, for he did his best to recover himself. "Let's not worry yet, lad. We'll ask around to see if anyone has seen him."

By now women and children were running up from the village looking for their men. Aunt Agnes was first among 'em, carrying her doctor's bag. Her face was set in a grim expression, but she sighed with relief when she saw us. She didn't say a word, just buried her head in Uncle Jim's shoulder and pulled me to the two of 'em.

"Well, now, what have you done to yourself?" she said once she broke away and got a look at Uncle Jim. She cleaned his wound and stitched it up. Then she was off to tend anyone else who needed her.

It was near dark, and the rescuers was still digging through the rubble. They brought out the dead on planks of wood and set up a little morgue right on the snow. Clyde's mother was there, too, but I couldn't bear to look at her. She was stricken with worry, and I kept my eyes down whenever she was near.

There were too many folks for Belton, so he was up the mountain, watching and hiding. I caught sight of him darting from one tree to another. For some reason, he warn't wearing coat or shoes. He was just a thin, white figure in the bare trees, and it made me think of Meek Jones disappearing into the woods the night he drowned.

An hour went by, maybe more, but in the end, the rescue workers brought out poor Clyde on a plank of wood. His body was whole, but one side of his little head was crushed. Mrs. Light fell to her knees in the snow. Belton came running, but the rescuers wouldn't let him near. It made me angry when folks said Belton didn't have no sense. He knew his brother was dead.

CHAPTER TWENTY

UNCLE JIM AND I POSTPONE REPAIRING THE BARN *and* ONCE AGAIN *I Do Some Spying* *at Night*

"Pass me the pencil, lad."

It was cold in the barn, and the lantern hanging on the bent nail above us hardly gave enough light. But we kept working. The job had to be done by morning. We stamped our feet to keep the feeling in 'em. Aunt Agnes gave me a pair of her gloves with the fingertips cut off so I could hold the nails easier.

Uncle Jim held up a plank of wood against me and

measured my height. He gave it another few inches since I was shorter than Clyde. The company store had run out of coffins. Besides, Mrs. Light didn't have the money for one. Coppers's stall and the gate to the barn would have to wait another year.

I hammered the sides together, trying to make it match just right for Clyde.

"Do you think we'll have time to paint it white?" I asked.

"We're going to try, lad. The night's on our side, for it's crisp and dry without a threat of snow."

All the Polish miners, plus a foreman and Clyde died in the collapse—nineteen total, the biggest mining accident in Holly Glen's history. I thought for sure the town would fold up and disappear, but it didn't. After the rescue team pulled out all the bodies, another crew went in to clean up the rubble and set up some new timbers, and the mine was open in another day. The whistle blew at dawn, and we headed off with our lunch pails. Markel stomped with pleasure when he saw me. I gave him some dried apple from my lunch pail and scratched him good and long between the ears. It was a regular day, as if nothing at all had happened and no one had died. The whistle blew again and we headed home. The only thing out of the ordinary was the announcement posted at the entrance—out of respect for the dead and their families, Mr. Newgate had cancelled the annual Christmas party. And even though my twelfth birthday was soon, I didn't feel much like celebrating that either.

After the paint dried, Uncle Jim and I carried the coffin to the boardinghouse. Aunt Agnes was there, helping Mrs. Light wash Clyde's body and get it ready for the funeral. I didn't want to see his body again, so when Uncle Jim went inside to help 'em place Clyde in his coffin I waited outside.

Seemed to me I'd seen enough of death. It scared me more than the spirits I felt, since it could come up on you with such violence and suddenness. I sat on the front steps of the boardinghouse and looked up at the sky. It stared back at me, cold and blank.

All Holly Glen turned out for the funeral of the nineteen dead. Their coffins filled the front half of the church, and everyone but the families had to stand outside to pay their respects. Folks were wailing and crying, or else all stiff in their bones, as if they was afraid if they let themselves soften they'd fall apart and break.

When it was my turn to walk by Clyde's little white coffin, I placed my hand over where I thought his heart might be. Neva Shyrock said the newly dead were awful sad, but I couldn't feel any sadness coming from Clyde.

What's it like bein' dead? I asked him. But he didn't answer, and all I could feel was how the paint was still sticky, and the smell of it filled up my nose as I walked past. There warn't nothing of Clyde there in that chapel, nothing that I could feel or sense in any way. Then it occurred to me that maybe Clyde's spirit warn't so sad after all. Maybe he was already with his daddy.

One night after the funeral, when Aunt Agnes was still tending to Mrs. Light and Belton, Mr. Moon and some other men come after supper. They sat by the stove, smoking pipes and talking in whispers. No one told me to leave or paid any attention to me at all, so I hid in the shadows of the corner of the room and listened.

"There warn't no reason for those men to die," said one.

"Don't forget the boy—he warn't twelve years old, his head crushed by the rubble. All because the company refused to bring in new timbers."

It was snowing outside, and the wind was howling. It rustled through the shingles of the cabin, and I shivered in the draft.

"It was Newgate's greed that killed those men and that boy," said Mr. Moon. "We've got to strike, men. We've got to close down the mine so we hit Newgate where he hurts. Make him lose some of his precious money! That'll make him listen!"

"Aye," said one of the Welshmen, angry and fierce, "but the Russians won't stand with us, and the Italians won't either. They're too terrified of losing their jobs since they're new to this country and don't know where else to go for work. So, it's just us and the coloreds, and I don't know that I trust them."

"Save your fury," said Uncle Jim. "The gentleman from the UMW will be there tonight. Let's hear what he has to say before we jump."

Mr. Moon pulled out his pocketwatch. "It's time to go, chaps. The meeting is about to start."

The men forgot I was there. Uncle Jim didn't say good-bye or tell me to go to bed. He put on his coat and hat like the others and went out in the night.

I felt awful curious. I wanted to follow the men to the meeting and hear what the man from the UMW had to say. I figured I'd trail 'em to wherever they was meeting, then hide under a window and listen. It was one of my old tricks, and I wasn't at all scairt. I was good at spying in the night. I slipped onto the porch without slamming the door or stomping too hard, but quiet and easy as you please.

I sprinted up the hillside into the woods, parallel to the men so I could keep up with 'em without being noticed. Others joined them till there was twenty or more heading toward the far end of town. Up the mountain in the last row of houses was a little house set off from the others with two lanterns burning in the window. Someone knocked on the door, and when the last man was inside, I run down there, silent and quick. I crept around the back of the house and looked through the window.

There was arguing and fighting, but I couldn't make

out what was being said because everyone was speaking their own language and no one was listening to anyone. The Italians was yelling in their language, and the Romanians was yelling in theirs. One of the colored fellas pushed over his chair, and the Welshmen was huddled together and nodding but keeping quiet for now. It seemed like all hell was gonna break loose till the man from the United Mine Workers took off his cap and stood up. He was tall and slim, and he waited till everyone was quiet to speak. He spoke in a full voice, and even though it was muffled some by the window, I could make out every word.

"It's one big union. Not a separate one for colored and another for Italians and another for Welsh. It's a union of workers, because that's what we are—workers. Those of you who are white and native born and think Mr. Newgate is like you are wrong. He ain't like you. He ain't like anyone here. He's like the coal baron in Beckley and the coal baron in Eccles. He's like the bank owners in Charleston and New York and Boston, but he ain't like you. He don't care about your children. He don't care about your wives. He don't care if you lose a leg in the mine, or an eye, or your life. He don't care if your ten-year-old son goes to school, or if he has to work in the mine because you can't haul as much coal anymore and there ain't enough food on the table. All he cares about is the coal you shovel out of his mountain. . . .

"Now, the union does care about you, but it don't care where you was born. And it don't care what color your skin is, what type of prayers you say, or whether you pray at all. It don't care if you load ten tons a day or if you load two."

"But when does the strike begin? And how long till the UMW comes through with the tents and the rations?" It was Clayton, standing straight and tall as any grown man there. "For you know that we won't be on strike more than half a day before Mr. Newgate sends the Baldwin-Felts guards in and they'll drive out our families with guns. I've got my mother to take care of. . . ."

Once the word "strike" was uttered, folks started interrupting again and calling out to be heard. One of the Italian miners was translating to his friends, and it was right impossible to hear who was saying what. So I hitched myself up on the windowsill best as I could, only I slipped and pitched forward, and my head banged the window. Some folks heard it and told everyone to hush up. Men turned in their seats and looked toward me. I figured I'd better heel it outta there, but Clayton had already run out the front door. He grabbed me by the neck of my coat and hauled me into the house.

"Look who I got here! My apprentice, Billy Creekmore!"

"Billy!" yelled Uncle Jim. "What are you doing here, lad? Go home now and leave us alone."

"He might be a spy!" said one of the men. "We better question him."

The union man walked up to me and looked me in the eye. "Are you a spy, Billy Creekmore? Or are you a union man?"

"I ain't no spy!" I said. "I came to learn about the union. I wanna be a union man."

CHAPTER TWENTY-ONE

I Become A Union Man and *We Face Our First Battle with* MR. NEWGATE AND HIS GUARDS

The men gave me a big hurrah for joining, but a minute later they went back to their arguing. Folks had different ideas about what should go first on our list of demands. Most miners hated cribbing more than anything else, but others wanted the company to make the job safer. Mr. Moon had the idea that the company should send in inspectors every morning to check for gases and the timbers. Others said that cave-ins and explosions were all part of being a miner and that we should set our minds on getting more money. Round and round it went, and nothing much was accomplished.

Still, it felt awful important being there with the men. I didn't say anything, just spent my time listening, but I felt respected just the same. I was a union man, with a full vote and the chance to speak my mind if I wanted.

We left in groups of threes and fours, moving swiftly and keeping our voices low.

"No need to call attention to ourselves," Uncle Jim said when I asked why we were going home this way. "It's best not to wake up the mine boss in his fine house over there."

We got home and both of us were surprised to see Aunt Agnes. She was sitting by the stove, rocking back and forth.

"Well," she said to us as we walked in.

Uncle Jim hung up his hat and coat. "How's Margaret and Belton?"

"They're sleeping, thank Heaven. Resting at last. I see Billy's with you."

"That's right," he nodded.

Aunt Agnes turned to me. "Well, I expect you're nearly of age, now. Doing a man's job, aren't you, Billy?"

"Yes, ma'am, I reckon . . ."

"So I guess you're making a man's decisions. . . ."

"Yes, ma'am."

"Well . . ." She looked at me standing for another moment, then turned back to the fire.

And that was all. She never scolded Uncle Jim for letting me join the union or going to meetings.

A few days later, as we was walking to the mine, Uncle Jim and I saw a crowd of miners gathered by Luther Spence and his family. They was out in the street, huddling against the cold. Snow was falling on their bare heads, and the older child was barefoot, trying to crawl up into his daddy's arms. Men with guns were inside his home, throwing out chairs and clothes.

"It's the Baldwin-Felts agents," said Uncle Jim. "They're Mr. Newgate's hired guards. Don't let them see you."

He pushed me behind him, but I poked my head around anyway to get a look. Ida Spence had her newborn twins in her arms. Both of 'em was crying from cold, and the snow was falling in their little pink faces. The Baldwin-Felts men didn't pay no mind to the crowd watching. They kept loading the wagon with every single thing the Spences owned, breaking dishes by their feet to scare 'em and make the little boy cry harder.

"Get outta their house!" someone yelled. I looked over to see who was yelling. It was Clayton.

A Baldwin-Felts man came out the door and stood on the porch. "This house is the property of the Newgate Coal Company, and Mr. Spence, here, has broken the terms of his lease by joining the United Mine Workers."

"Well, let him keep his things! Don't break up his dishes like that!" yelled someone in the crowd.

The other guard walked out of the cabin with Ida's kettle in his hand. "We're claiming this here property as payment for the fines Mr. Spence incurred by joining the union."

"You guards ain't nuthin' but thugs!" yelled someone else. More folks started calling the guards ruffians, bullies, and thieves. Next thing you know, someone in the crowd threw a rock. Then someone else did, and someone else, until one of the guards reached in his pocket and pulled out a pistol. I don't know how many times he shot it into the air. Folks jumped and ran for cover, and the crowd dissolved into nothing. Uncle Jim pulled me behind one of the houses nearby, 'cause I was too shocked to move my feet or know which way to turn.

Some folks run off. Others, like Uncle Jim and me, hid behind houses to see what would happen next. When the house was empty, the Baldwin-Felts men walked the family to the depot where a train had just pulled in. They had their guns out the whole way, and one of 'em nudged Luther in the ribs with the barrel as he boarded the train to be dumped in a different coal town somewhere in Mingo County. They didn't have nothing but the clothes on their backs—no food or bottles for the babies, not a pot to cook in, nor a penny in a pocket. When the train pulled away, the guards headed back off to the boardinghouse, laughing and cussing.

None of us talked or moved till they was inside and the door closed. Slowly we came out, mumbling 'bout what happened, but keeping our voices low as we walked up the hill to the mine. Clayton caught up to me and Uncle Jim.

"There must be a spy, Mr. Berry," he said. "He's taking names at our meetings and passing them on to Mr. Newgate. Those guards are picking on Luther to give us all a scare."

"That's right, lad. You and Billy have to keep your ears open. Pay attention to any chap who keeps talking to you about the meeting or asks you to remind him of what we talked about and who was there. The spy will try to get information from the two of you. He'll figure you're too young to know what he's after."

Later on, when the whistle blew and we come outta the mine, we walked into a whole different world. There was Baldwin-Felts guards everywhere. They was on the loading platforms just outside the entrance, scattered along the hillside and the streets of the town. They carried rifles over their arms or walked bloodhounds back and forth. Some of the miners cursed and shook their fists at 'em. But I was all quivery, near shaking in my boots when I passed.

"Don't be afraid, lad," whispered Uncle Jim. "That's what they want, to make us afraid."

It was a gray evening, without wind or early stars, and the sky was dissolving into snow. It covered up our steps as we walked home. I heard something going pat-pat-pat ever so softly, but I didn't know if it was the snow hitting the ground or the blood pulsing in my ears.

The next morning, the Baldwin-Felts guards filled the town like an army, watching us as we walked to work, looking for any reason at all to shoot or set the dogs on us. They hung outside the company store and walked up and down the village streets. Their dogs leapt when we passed, pulling against their leashes, barking and snarling like they'd just as soon rip us to pieces.

When we came outta the mine that evening, Mr. Newgate himself was there, surrounded by guards. There was eight of 'em, holding rifles, and the two front guards was leading a bear on a leash! A bear! It walked ahead of 'em about five feet or so. They whooped at the bear to make it stand up and take a few steps. It tossed its head and growled, swiping at air with its claws. This made the dogs go crazy. They lowered down on their forelegs, their hackles raised and teeth bared, barking and howling till I wondered if maybe I had died and gone to the hell the snake-handling preacher at the orphanage warned us about.

But a funny thing happened. Instead of getting scared, I got angry. All of us did. Seeing Mr. Newgate in town flanked by his guards, with his fat belly near sticking out of his topcoat, only made us more resolved to shut down the mine until he paid us better and gave us safer conditions.

The man from the UMW struck out of town and camped out in a holler on the banks of Paint Creek. Some miners stopped coming regular to meetings, for it was altogether a dicier situation. We snuck out of town one by one or in twos. And there was plenty of scares, too. Someone would misjudge where the guard was on his rounds, or we'd hear gunfire at our backs. Plenty of times Uncle Jim would tell me to just freeze and not move a muscle till he could tell if the dogs was coming our way. We'd wait between trees, still as statues, wishing our breath didn't steam the way it did, our hearts pounding, our eyes and ears tuned tight and fierce just like we was animals hunted in the night.

The union man gave us counsel and told us the state of things in the other mining camps up and down Paint Creek and the Tug River. We was planning one big strike that would close all the mines nearby. That way the railroads and the banks would lose big money, too, since there'd be no coal to haul and no reason for the coal companies to pay 'em. And, if all the mines closed down, Mr. Newgate and the other coal barons would be hard pressed to bring in enough workers from down south to keep the mines going.

"And if you're scared of dying, if you think we're pushing too hard, and demanding too much, remember that long ago Mr. Newgate decided he'd rather let men die than lose money. To save the cost of a few timbers, he let those men and that boy die. To save money in wages, he makes you work eleven hours instead of eight, letting you fill your lungs with coal dust, so that you're an old man at thirty, sitting by the fire coughing yourself to death. Sure, he brought his guards into town, and they're ready to shoot to kill. But if you think about it, you'll realize he's always been willing to kill, long as it helped him make a profit."

I didn't have to think about it. I knew the UMW man was right.

Long after midnight, taking different paths and leaving at different times, we headed back to our homes. Clayton shepherded different groups as we got closer to town. He headed out first after the meeting was done, then hung near the edge of town to watch the guards, holding us back or hurrying us on so we'd get back safe.

CHAPTER TWENTY-TWO

THE BALDWIN-FELTS GUARDS OPEN FIRE, and *My World Forever Changes*

It was spring. The snows melted and the trees were filling out with green. We gathered at the camp in the holler for our meetings, and Clayton was our guide. He called like a bobwhite if the coast was clear, whooping like a whippoorwill if the guards was coming our way. We were getting ready for the day the strike would begin. The UMW sent rations and tents, and we set them up in the woods, for sure enough we knew we'd be run outta town soon as the strike begun. We was preparing for the long haul, and aiming to shut down all the mines in the Tug River Valley. Every day Mr. Newgate lost money, said the UMW man, brought us closer to our goals.

It was joyful in a way, exciting the way telling my stories used to be. Knowing there was a spy about kept me on my toes, but even this added some fun. I loved tipping my hat to Mr. Wheeton in the morning, and dropping my eyes when I passed a Baldwin-Felts man like I was ever so scared. I'd even fake a tremble if they yelled at me to look an elder in the eye.

"Yes, sir," I'd say and look at 'em like I was 'bout to burst into tears. But inside my heart was cold and glad, glad I could fool 'em and go about on the sly, working for the union and planning our strike.

It was in the middle of the night, sometime in April with the sky sprinkled with stars. We was stocking boxes of canned food in a tent in the woods. A lantern hung above us. Clayton, Uncle Jim, Mr. Moon, and I were working together; other folks in other tents, not far off, doing the same. Clayton heard the first shot.

"Listen up!" he said. "I heard gunfire." His words were barely out when I heard it, too, and then there was more. We heard footsteps running, and miners yelling out to one another. You could hear dogs in the distance and the sound of wood breaking, like maybe they was taking a hatchet to the tents or else breaking through trees.

"Get outta the tents!" a voice yelled at us. "It's the Baldwin-Felts and they're coming for us! They're shooting up the camp!" Clayton tore open the tent flap and out in the night we went running. I could hear the dogs and see some of the guards running with torches and guns. Shots broke out, and one bullet whizzed past me, sounding like the singe of a match. Outta the corner of my eye, I saw Uncle Jim fall.

"Keep running, Billy!" yelled a voice. It was Clayton. I turned to see him kneeling by Uncle Jim, who was laid out on the ground, his chest covered in blood.

"Don't stop, Billy! Keep running!"

Another bullet whizzed by, and I saw Clayton jerk backward. His body was spread out not far from Uncle Jim's. I didn't have to get close to know both of 'em was dead.

I ran through the woods, my heart bursting, my lungs feeling like they was being stabbed with knives. I ran away from the gunshots, the dogs barking, and men yelling in the night. I picked up one path then abandoned it for another. It was two miles or more into Holly Glen, and I ran the whole way. I tore open the front door, and Aunt Agnes rose from her chair when she saw me.

"What, Billy? What is it, boy?"

"They shot Uncle Jim. . . . They shot him and he fell . . . and Clayton bent down to be with him, but he told me to keep runnin', and both of 'em are dead. . . ." The words near broke me, my chest was heaving and aching so, and then I started bawling, and I couldn't stop till Aunt Agnes put her hands on my shoulders and shook me a little.

"Stop it, Billy. You've got to stop crying and keep your wits about you. You've got to run away now, 'cause soon the guards'll be coming into town and rounding up all of you that's run off. . . . And there'll be more shooting and more killing, and they'll be after you 'cause you're in the union, so you've got to leave now. . . ."

It was like she had been expecting this all along and had decided long ago what to do once the shooting started. In a flash she pulled together a sack of food and supplies. She packed a knife, and some rope, a couple bottles of her medicines, and an old sheet to rig up a tent from a tree.

"Follow the train tracks to Charleston," she said.

"Ain't it dangerous for you to stay? Shouldn't you come with me?"

"I'm no threat to Mr. Newgate and his guards. I'm just a woman. I don't work in his mines and I can't join the union. But you're a union man, one that's already planning strikes, and he'll be out to get you, so you've gotta leave."

"Come with me. I'm too afraid to go alone."

"I can't, Billy. I'd only slow you down. Besides, the best thing I can do for folks is stay here and help tend those that's been hurt. You've got to go now, before the guards set on the town. Now don't forget these . . ."

She took the postcards and broken necklace out of my old tin and put them in the bag.

"I'm lost to you now for you can't ever come back

here. There's only your father now, and you must find him if you can."

I took the bag from her, then she hugged me tight for a moment. "Keep moving, Billy. Put as many miles between you and Holly Glen as you can."

And so I left. I turned my back on Holly Glen and the only home and family I ever had. I tore down the footpath along the tracks outta town, not knowing where I was going or if I'd ever see Aunt Agnes again. I don't know how long I kept running, only that dawn came and went and I was still on my feet, only slower now so I could keep going without my heart giving out.

Part Three

CHAPTER TWENTY-THREE

ALONE IN THE WOODS *a Different Type of* SPIRIT COMES TO ME

For weeks I lived in the woods, finding shelter in rundown guard stations near the switches or else under the boughs of a tree with the sheet Aunt Agnes give me spread above. My clothes got to be all rags and dirt. Days was mostly sunshiny and still with the faint dronings of bugs in the air that can drive a body crazy. If I listened too hard, I'd start wishing I was dead, for it was an agitating sound that made me think of Uncle Jim and Clayton dying in the hollow, and the evilness of the guards running through the camp with their guns. There was spirits all about, but they were ancient and proud, not the newly dead filled with yearning to find their kin. They kept their distance, and the only thing I felt from them was indifference.

I kept a move on best I could, hoping Charleston would appear soon. There were more switches than I ever thought, with tracks branching off to the northeast or southeast, as well as some that just seemed to circle back to nowhere. But where I was actually heading, I couldn't say. Nights was lonely and long, with possum and raccoons creeping through the underbrush and scaring me so I could hardly sleep. I don't think a human had stepped foot in those parts since the Chesapeake and Ohio first laid tracks fifty years ago.

One afternoon a grand train with seventy cars or more, loaded with coal, carrying timber and passenger cars, rumbled by. I heard it coming a mile away, and saw its smoke rising above the tree line. It passed too fast for me to see the folks looking out the window, but

I wondered about 'em. Where was they going, and what was they after? Was they miners or their kin? I thought about folks back in Holly Glen, and it almost tore me up not knowing how my aunt Agnes was, or Clyde's mother, or little Belton. I wondered who'd bring Uncle Jim's and Clayton's bodies back to town for a funeral and who would help Aunt Agnes in her grieving.

Days run together, and then one morning in a wide part of the valley, I came upon a string of ten cars or more on a siding off the main line. They was waiting to be picked up by a locomotive, I reckoned. Some were flat cars carrying the longest poles I'd ever seen, and some were box and passenger cars. All in all, it warn't like any train I'd ever seen. A few of the cars carried blue and gold wagons, and the sun picked up the glittery paint, and the shine sparkled my eyes. Down yonder from the tracks off in the trees was a whole crowd of folks, some lounging on blankets in little groups here and there, and others fishing in the creek. As I got closer, I could see posters with painted pictures and fancy script covering the sides of a few of the front cars. Suddenly, I realized plain as day that it was a circus train. I got to where I could read the posters and one of 'em said:

CHARLES SPARKS
WORLD FAMOUS CIRCUS!
Now in Its 30th Year!!!

I started running up to the folks under the tree, whooping hello and waving my hat to 'em. Some of the folks stood up with a jump, and I guess I must have looked awful wild and strange, running out from the woods, my face covered in dirt and my clothes all raggedy.

"Are you real circus folks?" I yelled. I was excited as could be, remembering how glorious the circus in Charleston was, and what a fine time I had with Uncle Jim and Clyde.

"We sure are, son," said a man. "Who might you be and where are you from?" He was straight and elegant as you please, with a royal sounding voice. I guessed right away he was the ringmaster.

"I'm Billy Creekmore, and I'm not from anywhere." Then before I could think to stop myself, and probably because I hadn't had a soul to talk to in so long, the words tumbled out of me and I told him my life story. I went on and on, not knowing what to leave out, so I didn't leave out much. I told him about my mother's death and my pa's postcards, the way Mr. Beadle beat us and how I just barely escaped the glass factory. I talked about Rufus and Peggy, Aunt Agnes and Uncle Jim, Clyde Light and his little brother with his strange ways, and Clayton and the union man, then how the Baldwin-Felts guards shot my uncle and my friend, and how I didn't know what town they was visiting next, but they better stay clear of Holly Glen. Somewhere in the story, I started crying and it felt like my heart was breaking when I told them about my uncle, Clayton, and Clyde.

Other folks had come around to listen. Some were sinewy and strong, some were beautiful as kings and queens, and others had the funniest kind of bodies, all pear shaped or uneven on one side. One fellow came up to my waist, tiny as could be, but muscled like a strong man. There was an Oriental family of tumblers that I recognized from one of the posters, and a fat lady all soft and billowy in her flesh. All of 'em had kind faces.

"Well, Bert, let's take him along!" said the fat lady. Tears were streaming down her face. "Let him ballyhoo to earn his keep till we teach him an act or give him a trade. But don't leave the poor little orphan behind!"

Others took up the cry, and it warn't no time at all before Bert said all right, and it was fine by him for they could use another boy posting bills, 'cause it was too much work for the one little guy they had. Bert gave me a clean cloth and told me to go rinse off by the creek, then he gave me some clean overalls to put on. Other folks shared their lunch with me. It was cold fried chicken and pickled eggs, and I think I shocked everyone with how quick I gobbled it up.

Before long, a locomotive come by on the main track. It slowed to a stop just where the siding meets the main track. Someone ran down to wake up the trainmaster, who was still sleeping under a tree, and soon enough the engineer and him was shaking hands and saying howdy do, and thanks for coming along. A band of men hooked up the circus train to the locomotive and double-checked everything before we set off. I sat in the passenger car in a little sliver of a space next to the fat lady. Her name was Darla and wasn't it a wonder, she said, that I lived in the woods for so long without a grown-up and wouldn't I like life in the circus so much more.

"Sure, I will," I said. "Back in Charleston I saw the Frederick Ainsworth Circus in a show 'bout King Solomon and the Queen of Sheba and there was the most darin' trick riders, just as elegant and carefree as can be. . . ."

"And did your pockets get picked, and was you shortchanged at the ticket booth? Did folks living nearby get their washings stole right off their clotheslines, for I've heard terrible things about that circus. Filled with scoundrels and thieves, s'what they say. A regular con man's show . . ."

"Oh, no," I said. "Nothin' like that happened, and, oh, it was a right spectacle, ever so glorious, set back in ancient Egypt times, and . . ."

"That's all right. I don't want to hear it," Darla said, fluttering her hand in the air like she was warding off a swarm of flies. "Mr. Ainsworth's got a low-class show, not a thing like ours, and don't he treat his folks bad? Why, you just ask Mr. Paul Wenzel who conducts the clown band. He used to do the same for that Mr. Ainsworth, and don't he have plenty of stories to tell. . . ."

I felt awful worried that I made her cross, so I did my best to make things better. "Oh, well, the clowns was just awful! And so was the trapeze artist. He fell down a dozen times or more, then the fire-eater near burned off a lady's hair!"

This pleased her considerable. She looked out the window, happy as pie to hear about all the things that went wrong.

"Oh, you'll like it with us," she said, smiling. "It's a Sunday type show, clean as can be, entertaining the folks with spectacles and feats without cheating a soul. And Mr. Sparks loves us like family, feeds us like family, too, and you'll have a family with us, if you want. Didn't Mr. Sparks take on that other little boy? Of course, he did! You'll meet Mr. Sparks soon. He's with the advance crew in Huntington, meeting the mayor and fixing our parade route through town. Oh, he's a wonderful man!"

She went on and on, chattering away, till all of a sudden she fell asleep, just like that, her head knocking the window with every little bump on the rails, and her great body sliding across the seat and shoving me into the aisle.

"Did she faint?" I asked the man sitting across from her.

"No, that's just Darla's way of falling asleep. She's resting up for the parade and tonight's show. Come on and sit here. There's a space for you." And so I sat next to Jimmie Carroll, who played trombone in the Big Show Band with his pa and near twenty other fellas. He was born in the very train we was on and had worked the Sparks Circus all his life. Seemed like he loved talking, too. I tried paying attention, but my mind drifted back to Holly Glen. I could see Aunt Agnes stoking the fire alone in the cabin. Of all the women she helped in their grieving, I wondered which one was with her now.

CHAPTER TWENTY-FOUR

The CHARLES SPARKS CIRCUS Takes Me Under Its Wing *and* I MAKE A CONFESSION TO A FRIEND

We pulled into Huntington, and folks jumped off the train right and left, helping to unload things, or running off to meet up with other folks. Darla took me by the hand and waddled through what looked like pure chaos to me.

"It ain't chaos," she corrected me. "Ain't nothing like it. Pretty soon the cookhouse will be serving lunch, the Big Top will be up, and we'll be getting in our costumes for the parade. Now, you just put on your best manners 'cause I'm taking you to meet Mr. Sparks."

We walked among the hammer gang, the roustabouts, all of 'em busy spreading out the vast canvas tenting and attaching the ends to stakes they pounded into the ground with sledgehammers near big as me. Darla stepped between ropes regal as a queen, and none of the men had a thing to say about it. They yelled plenty at me, though, telling me to look where I was going and didn't I see how I tangled up the lines, and so forth. Just beyond the huge spread of the Big Top, I could see the lions in their cages and four elephants chained to a post by their back legs. They was eating hay while one fella scrubbed 'em with a long-handled brush. Another man in a blood-stained apron was carrying a side of cow ribs to the lions. He was the circus butcher. Darla said that one of the trains was filled with livestock that he butchered on the road to feed man and beast alike. Well, like any other boy would, I bolted over there to see the lions eat, but Darla yanked me back.

"What if one of the supervisors or Mr. Sparks himself

sees you wandering about? They'd think you snuck in for free, then they'd throw you out. And there you'd be—off on your own! An orphan again!"

By and by, Darla spotted Mr. Sparks going over a clipboard of notes with some other men. It looked awful official to me, but Darla warn't one bit afraid. "They're just the managers, don't let them worry you. I'm a performer, and Mr. Sparks always speaks to me, no matter how busy he is. Oh, Mr. Sparks! Mr. Sparks!" She waved to him, bold as can be. "I want you to meet somebody. . . ."

Mr. Charles Sparks excused himself, then turned to Darla with a little bow. He was dark haired and clean-shaven, and he wore a bow tie and a ruby ring. "Why, Darla," he said, "what a pleasure." He bent down and kissed her hand. "And who do you have here?"

"This here is Billy Creekmore, and he come running out of the woods this morning, raggedy and dirty, without food or shelter, and no family to speak of. He's just a lonely little orphan boy, Mr. Sparks! One of the world's castaway children. Just like I was when my parents left me to fend for myself on the streets of Chicago, without home or family till the day I joined the sideshow of the Sparks Circus. . . . Now, don't you think we can find a place for him here?"

Mr. Sparks stepped back a little to give me the once over, but he warn't trying to scare me, only to size me up, I reckon.

"Well, we might be able to find him a place. . . . What's your sense of him, Darla? Is he an honest boy? A good worker?"

"Oh, I think so, Mr. Sparks. . . ."

"Then it all depends on Billy and whether he's willing to work hard for the circus. Can you do that, Billy?"

"Why, yes sir, Mr. Sparks. I've been workin' hard all my life, first at the orphanage farm and then at the mine. I was a mule skinner in the Newgate Mine over in Holly Glen. . . ."

"You don't say . . . ," said Mr. Sparks. His face brightened a bit, and he nodded to me all respectful. "We can always use help with the mules and the horses. The vet and the blacksmith have more than they can handle. But first, I need you to work the advance. You'll be with another boy, going into towns a couple weeks ahead of the circus, pasting up posters, then meeting back up with us to check in and get more supplies. What do you say to that, Billy?"

My heart sank. Here I was, hoping to be on the road to becoming a trick rider. I could see the pony boys brushing the stallions and braiding their manes for the parade. The riders were adjusting their headpieces and fastening their capes. I had to stop myself from sighing out loud.

"Uh, sir . . . What I'd really like is to be a trick rider."

"Well, son, I can't promise that. If you work out, we can see about getting you some training. But right now I need someone to work the advance. That is, if you want to join the circus . . ."

"Thanks, sir." I sighed, hoping he was a man of his word. "I'd be happy to."

"Good. Now, let me introduce you to your supervisor, Matthew, and the other boy who works with him. Where's that new boy? Someone send him over here to meet Billy."

Well, if I said that my eyes nearly dropped out of my head, I wouldn't be exaggerating much, for who comes darting out of the crowd but Rufus Twilly! He took one look at me and just about fainted dead away himself.

"Billy! Billy Creekmore!" he cried out, and ran toward me with open arms. We swung each other around, laughing. Mr. Sparks chuckled, saying something about how the circus reunites folks with a shared past, but I can't remember the particulars. My mind was still dazed and jumpy from things.

Matthew introduced himself, then the three of us headed over to the advance car. It was jam packed from floor to the ceiling. A lithograph machine was bolted to one side of the car, and three sleeping berths were lined up on the other, all stacked up on each other. In between were stacks of paper and buckets of paint, so there was hardly any room to walk.

Before long, a little locomotive came along and picked us up. Then we were off, crossing the Ohio River to three towns I'd never heard of before—Ironton, Portsmouth, and Cincinnati. Matthew ran the press for a while, printing up a few hundred posters, then he crawled into the bottom bunk and was snoring away within a minute. Seemed like circus folk could take a nap anytime, anyplace, without any need to get drowsy or to wake up slowly. The air in our car was filled with a clean type of smell that reminded me of laundry day in Holly Glen. Rufus said it was the ink. He went over the route with me on a big railroad map he kept in his pocket. The towns crossed off in red were ones he and Matthew had already visited. He folded back the map and pointed to a town just up the Cheat River from Albright.

"This here is Morgantown, where the glassworks is. I was sittin' in Mr. Colder's car, on my way to be an apprentice in his factory. We had stopped at a fillin' station to get some gas, and just over yonder I could see the roustabouts settin' up the Big Top. I don't know what came over me, but all of a sudden I decided I'd open the door and sneak out. Heck, Mr. Colder didn't even notice. He was too busy arguin' with the attendant over his change. By the time he got back in the car I was long gone."

"You don't say, Rufus. That was awful darin' of you."

"Peggy gave me the idea. Soon as I heard I was goin' to be apprenticed, she started helpin' me figure out how to run away. She was dead set against me going to the glassworks. Said I'd get maimed or die for sure. The next Sunday she was in Albright goin' to church when she saw posters for the Sparks Circus performance in Morgantown. She told me to look for the Big Top when Mr. Colder drove into town so I could run off and find it soon as I had a chance. Only I never made it to the dormitory. Never even saw it or the factory."

I was right impressed with Rufus, and I told him so.

It was almost two hundred miles to Ironton, Ohio, and we passed the time trading stories and catching up. He reckoned his pa was still in jail, and he was awful sad to hear that I didn't have no way of getting word to my father 'bout where I was. All in all, Rufus hadn't changed much. He was taller and fuller, with some muscles in his arms from carrying rolls of posters and buckets of paint all over, but he was still sunny in nature and freckled all over.

"You're different, though," he told me. "I'd say you're sadder. Maybe you've been seein' too many spirits. Maybe you're burdened by all those birds tellin' you who's gonna die next. . . ."

My stomach tightened up, like I had just swallowed something with an awful taste. I took a deep breath.

"No, it ain't that," I said. "All those times I said birds was talkin' to me was just a lie. I just made that stuff up, either to get outta trouble or else to tell a good story."

"Well, you don't say," said Rufus. "You sure fooled plenty of folks. Includin' me. Don't you ever see spirits?"

"Sometimes I feel 'em. Only they're not speakin' in words, and they're not evil or scary. They're sad mostly."

"What kinda spirits are they, then?"

"I think they're the spirits of folks that's been killed before their time. Back in Holly Glen, I felt two spirits. One was the father of a friend of mine who died, and the other was the first boy that was killed in the Newgate Mine. His name was Golden Breedlove, and he used to follow me in the mine. Lots of times I'd feel him near me. Other folks did, too. He was awful sad, wanderin' about hopin' someone would lead him outta the mine to his mother."

"So, all those times at the orphanage, you was mostly actin'?"

"No, I wouldn't exactly say that, although I was

actin' some of the time. . . . Lookin' back on it, I think I was sensin' spirits that was roamin' about the place, only I didn't know it then. Remember the graveyard on the hill behind the chapel? Remember all the little crosses with the names of the boys who had died at the orphanage?"

"Sure I do. Meek Jones is buried up there. So's lots of boys."

"Right . . . well, remember how their names had worn away from snowstorms and rain? I bet all those boys wanted someone to remember 'em and the hard life they led, so they spoke to me when I was wanderin' about at night, only I didn't know it. I'd be out lookin' at the moon or havin' a walk to think things over, then I'd feel somethin' sad and lonely driftin' through the trees like mist. I used to think I was missin' my parents, feelin' sorry for myself 'cause I didn't have a family. I guess I was partly right, but now I think I was feelin' the spirits of the boys at the orphanage who died from hardship and neglect. Darla called me a castaway child, and said she was one, too, before she joined the circus. Maybe the spirits I feel are the ghosts of castaway children. But I've never really seen a ghost or heard one. Mostly, it's a feelin' I get when I'm in certain places."

It was the first time I had really put these thoughts together, and they surprised me as much as they did Rufus. I guess all those days alone in the woods gave me the time and place to figure out a few things.

Rufus was awful quiet for a while. I couldn't tell if he was angry with me for lying back in the orphanage or angry with me for telling the truth now. He stared out the window or studied the map, keeping to himself without looking at me or starting up another conversation. Finally he said something, which relieved me considerable since I didn't know what else to say.

"Mr. Sparks is a different sort of person than Mr. Beadle or Mr. Colder," he said. "And workin' in the Sparks Circus is different, too. There ain't no ghosts lingerin' about, and no one beats on any of the children or makes 'em do things that are too dangerous for a grown-up. We're fed well, too. The tables in the dinin' tent is covered with tablecloths, and there's waiters to serve us, and they's treated well themselves, although they always eat last. But all in all, the Sparks Circus is a family, and I think you'll like it here. You won't have to pretend you see a spirit to get outta bein' mistreated like you did."

I was downright chagrined, embarrassed and comforted at the same time. "I never told a lie to be mean," I said.

"I know. I've always known you ain't a mean person. I can tell a mean person a mile off," said Rufus. "Seems to me you got two talents—tellin' stories and sensin' spirits, and sometimes you mix 'em up."

"I guess so," I answered. "Only I've got things more settled in my mind now. I don't think I'll mix 'em up no more, either on purpose or by accident."

After a couple of hours, the train pulled our car onto a sidetrack outside the depot, and like magic Matthew woke up. He stretched his arms in big circles and twisted at the waist a few times. An engineer from the yard came over to uncouple our car from the main train.

"Come on, boys," Matthew said, smiling. He liked his job. "We've got two hours to paper this town before we get on the train to Portsmouth."

We picked up our posters and buckets and jumped off the train.

"You take the road along the river, Billy, and Rufus, you take the main road into town. I'll take the roads behind the jail. Here you go . . . take these free tickets and give 'em to any store owner that lets you paper his store. And don't paper any houses or churches since it's disrespectful. Be back at the depot by three and don't be late."

The three of us papered every wall and fence we could see. There was a parade on the poster, with a band of clowns playing banjos and horns, then came Darla sitting on a float drawn by white horses with lions roaring about, and finally came the Ling family walking on their hands and turning flips in the air. By the end of the two hours, my arms were aching from all the hauling and pasting I was doing, and I near crawled back to the advance car. Rufus and Matthew were already there, resting on their berths waiting for me.

"You've got to rest when you can," said Matthew, letting his head tilt back and his hat fall over his eyes. "When you're with a circus, the work never stops." I crawled up to my berth, but I couldn't sleep none since my nose near touched the top of the car. It took me a few days, but I got used to it.

Later on we joined up to another train that took us to Portsmouth, and Cincinnati. We papered both towns from the barns on the outskirts to the gates of the floodwalls, and everything in between. Rufus even climbed up a rickety ladder to paste a poster on the watertower by the fire station. He was trying to get used to heights, just in case he decided to become a tightrope walker.

"Usually, you are born into performin', but Mr. Sparks lets us kids have a try, if we want. First we have to work for a year, either in the advance crew, or in the kitchen, but after that, he lets us train to be clowns or performers, if we want. What do you want to be, Billy?"

"A trick rider. Had my heart set on it ever since I saw the circus with my uncle Jim and my buddy Clyde."

"Now that'll be tough. . . . The Christiani family has that pretty well tied up, seein' how they have five kids. Why, that family's been trick riders all the way back to olden times. Been performin' for all those kings and queens in Europe since the time of King Louis Fifteen."

I got a little discouraged hearing this, but I figured if I did a good enough job on the advance crew, maybe Mr. Sparks would ask them to give me a try.

"Say!" said Rufus. "I know the perfect job for you! You could work the sideshow as a fortune-teller! Why, you're a natural, seein' how you're so good with words and makin' up stories."

"Nah, I don't wanna be a fortune-teller." His words stung me a little, to tell the truth. I didn't want Rufus to think of me as someone who could look into someone's face and make up a story 'bout themselves. It was too much like lying for money, and it didn't appeal to me. "Right now I'm happy ridin' trains from town to town and pastin' up posters for the show."

"Oh, ballyhooin's fun all right. I ain't sayin' it ain't fun," said Rufus. "You get to travel about, and you're on your own mostly. But you get restless for somethin' else, especially since there's so many fun jobs at the circus. You'll see."

"I guess I will," I answered. I didn't want to talk about it anymore, so I agreed with him.

We worked all day papering three towns and catching four different trains. I learned how to work the lithograph machine, and when it warn't running, Rufus and I stirred the paste to keep it from getting solid.

We backtracked to Huntington, where the circus was already over and the roustabouts were taking down the Big Top. It was dark when we got there, but it warn't at all quiet. Different groups of folks was walking about here and there, helping each other pack up or finish their job. The kitchen tent was long gone to the next town, but Matthew found Rufus and me some sandwiches and a plate of cold beans to share. The lions was growling in their cages, waiting to be fed, and the little boys in the Ling family were chasing each other in the dark while their mother was calling to 'em in Chinese. A group of clowns walked by. Their makeup was off and the only reason I knew they was clowns was because there was a little white greasepaint behind the one fella's ear. Some of 'em was fat, and some of 'em was thin, and you could tell their bodies was awful nimble and could do whatever they wanted, like walking a pretend tightrope or dancing soft shoe, or acting tipsy, or bowing very dainty like they was at court before a king.

Matthew found Mr. Sparks and told him I was a good worker who did his job just fine. Mr. Sparks still had his clipboard in his hand, but he took time out to look me in the eye and shake my hand. He asked me if I liked the job all right, and I said yes, I did. Then he said very good and welcomed me to the Sparks World Famous Circus.

CHAPTER TWENTY-FIVE

We Paper Towns All over Wisconsin, AND *I Meet Up with Another Person from My Past*

Well, the weeks run along, and it was the beginning of summer now. I got used to the routine of circus life, the early risings and the long days, passing through small towns and big towns with my posters and paste. Matthew worked us hard, but never had no harsh word for Rufus and me. Only an urging now and then to hurry up 'cause the train was coming soon, and we hadn't even papered the center of town. We passed through well-kept towns filled with churches and banks and shiny stores, and tackety ones with wooden buildings aching for new paint and a window wash. There was smoky mill towns that smelled bad and grim little coal camps that reminded me of Holly Glen. Sometimes I saw children climbing a hill of coal near the tracks, stealing coal for the stove at home, and sometimes I saw boys my own age heading back from the mine, their faces black with dust. A kind of sadness came over me, almost like I longed to be living that type of life again. I'd look at 'em and think about Aunt Agnes, Belton, and Mrs. Light, wondering if the strike was cancelled and if the Baldwin-Felts men was still there, watching their every move. I didn't dare write Aunt Agnes yet, but I so longed to tell her about the life I was leading now. If only Uncle Jim knew! He'd be so happy for me, seeing how much he loved the circus himself.

We was way up north in Wisconsin, three days ahead of the circus train. I was printing up some posters, and Rufus was setting them to dry on the rows of shelves built in the side of the car.

"Say, Billy," he said, "I was thinkin' you and I should tell Mr. Sparks we want to be clowns. Don't you think we'd have a heck of a time bein' clowns? We could work the crowd between the acts, pickin' folks outta the audience and playing tricks on 'em, like gettin' 'em to play catch with us, only the ball would be a balloon full a paint and it'd pop on 'em and spoilt their clothes."

"Why, Rufus Twilly, how you talk! Just what makes you think Mr. Sparks would let any of his clowns act like that? You know he runs a good show that don't cheat or take 'vantage of folks."

Sun was pouring through the windows and we was making good time. There warn't no mountains up here, only layers of smooth hills and dark blue lakes. We were on our way to Rush City, Rice Lake, and White Bear Lake, which struck my curiosity since I thought there warn't any white bears 'cept way up north where it snowed all the time. I didn't think Wisconsin was anywhere near the Arctic, but I warn't sure and Rufus warn't either. We couldn't ask Matthew since he was taking his usual nap.

"I'm just thinkin', Billy, just thinkin' 'bout what type

of trainin' I want once my year of workin' advance is up come October. I've got my heart set on bein' a clown."

"Well, I've set my sights on bein' a trick rider."

"I don't know, Billy. I still think you'd be awful good tellin' fortunes."

"Nyah, I don't wanna do that. Say, who knows . . . maybe one of those Christiani kids will wanna be a trapeze artist instead. Then I could take his spot."

We papered Rush City and Rice Lake, but it was another eighty-three miles to White Bear Lake, so I managed to take a nap myself. It was after seven when we got there, but the sun was still up since we were far enough north to have those long summer days when the sun don't stay down for more than a few hours every day. White Bear Lake was a good-sized town with four streets crisscrossing like the spokes of a wagon wheel through the center, so there was plenty of fences and walls and sides of buildings to cover. Lots of folks were out walking the wooden sidewalks along the edge of the lake, and they stopped to read the dates and look at the picture soon as I got a poster pasted up. Kids pulled at their parents and whined to go, and I could tell there'd be a good turnout for the show.

By the time the sun was down, I was heading back to the depot to meet up with Matthew and Rufus. My shoulders were aching from all that pasting. I was barely lifting my feet I was so tired, but I couldn't help looking through town as I walked, wondering 'bout the folks who lived there. It was a clean town, with all the storefronts crisp and neat without any missing letters on the windows. All the lampposts along Main Street were hung with baskets of red flowers, and down the way a friendly lookin' fella was lightin' the gas.

I rounded a corner when I spied a fella looking at a poster I put up an hour ago. Only he warn't reading the poster, he was peeling it off. The paste was still wet and it came off in one piece. He crumpled up the poster and threw it to the ground. Then he took one of his own posters from a stack by his feet, and stuck it up where mine had been. I watched him walk down the road a bit and do the same to a poster I had put up on the side of a dry goods store, and he was on his way to another. I near exploded with anger and ran up to him.

"Hey, mister!" I yelled. "What are you doin' to my posters?"

The man was tall and lanky with an angular face that I could barely make out in the dark. He leaned against the wall and sized me up with a cool look on his face. "Your posters? Are you Mr. Charles Sparks hisself?"

"No, I ain't, but I work for him, and he pays me to put up his posters. Now you're takin' 'em down."

Just then, Rufus come running up to me yelling hello and was I finished and when exactly was the train coming and warn't I awful tired and warn't I hungry, too. He stopped dead in his tracks when he saw our crumpled up poster by the man's feet.

"Who are you?" asked Rufus. "And what are you doin' to our posters?"

"My friends call me Billy," he said. "I'm sure the three of us can be friends." He rustled in his pocket and held out two coins in the palm of his hand. "Now, why don't each of you take a silver dollar and run off. Go meet up with your supervisor and get on your train, but don't tell him nothing 'bout me. I won't take down any more of your posters. Go on now . . . take your money."

Rufus stepped forward, and for a second I thought he was gonna take the money, but it turned out his natural friendliness was taking over.

"Why, this here is Billy, too. Billy Creekmore, and I'm Rufus Twilly."

"Billy Creekmore?" The man stepped forward and took a long look at me. "Is that your name, boy? Let me see now . . ." He took my chin and tilted my face toward the light. "Yep, those are her eyes all right, blue eyes with black lashes. . . ."

I looked back at him. He was familiar in a way, only I warn't exactly sure how.

"Can't you guess who I am?" His face broke into a grin. "Can't you guess who's standing here before ya?"

It was beginning to dawn on me, but I was cold speechless, and it took Rufus to put out the words, for he guessed right away.

"Why, you're Billy's father!"

"That's right!" he cried, his eyes bright with tears. He burst out laughing, pulled me to his chest, and hugged me hard. "I'm your flesh and blood, your own pa!"

My own eyes filled up, too, but I couldn't really cry because everything was happening so fast it didn't seem real.

"Last I heard," he went on, "you was at that orphanage, getting an education and going to church. Now here we are in White Bear Lake, meeting up at long last. . . ."

"Billy and I work the advance for the Sparks Circus," said Rufus. "We're circus folk. But, say, what are you doin' to our posters? Our supervisor will be awful angry when he sees what you've done."

"Uh, now, boys. You see, I'm just doin' a little reconnaissance work for the circus I'm with. The Graftin Circus it's called, and Mr. Graftin's always been right impressed with your outfit. Says your posters are the best in the business, so he sent me to get a few so we could copy some of the ideas. Imitation is the best form of flattery, and don't you forget it. . . . But hey now, Billy, you're letting your friend do all the talking. Don't you have nothin' to say to your pa?"

"Well, then, why didn't you take down just one poster and keep it neat," Rufus went on, "instead of takin' down near every one we put up?"

But I wasn't thinking 'bout the posters no more. There I was standing with the father I'd been missing and longing for all these years. He smiled down at me while I fumbled for words. Finally something came to me. "I saved all the postcards you sent me."

"Did you? Well, then you got quite a collection, since I've been traveling all over the country, first with one circus then another. Been in every state east of the Mississippi, and even a few out west. Hope you kept 'em in good condition, for the stamps alone is worth lots of money. Heck, I'm awful glad to run into you like this. You're saving me a trip. I wasn't planning on coming to get you till you was thirteen, but I guess you're old enough as it is."

"Old enough for what?" I asked.

"To come with me and learn the trade, son. Oh, I've got lots of stuff to teach you, Billy. We'll travel the world and meet paupers and princes. Sleep under the stars some nights and in castles the others."

He clapped his hands and laughed at the sky. "Oh, son, the world's wide open to us! Adventures every day of the week. We could be a father-son act, 'cause if blood is blood then sure enough you're a natural for the sideshow just like me."

"That's just what I told him," said Rufus, all excited. "Why, you should hear Billy tell a story! He'd fool anyone, he's so full of detail. Just like it's all a memory, but it ain't! Turns out he made up most of the stories he used to tell back at the orphanage, includin' the ghosty ones! Right outta his head he got 'em, but he fooled me and everyone else who was listenin'!"

"Well, all this is good to know, good to know. Now, Billy, the Graftin Circus is considerable smaller than Mr. Sparks's outfit, less polished too. I can't say we have the fanciest acrobats or the shiniest costumes. To be true, it ain't nothing more than a mud show really, but there's always a place for new talent. And I can tell that's what you are, Billy. New talent!"

Right then, Matthew come along, and before anyone else could say a word, Rufus told him the situation, how we had run into my very own father and warn't that the most amazing thing, and how I was gonna leave with him now to go work the Graftin Circus, which my pa added was just across the state line, but was heading this way more or less.

"Heading this way more or less, eh?" said Matthew. "Heading this way exactly, I'd say. Bet you know our whole itinerary in these parts. Bet you're planning on posting over our bills and stealing our audience a day before we get to town. Oh, I know all about the Graftin Circus and how you do business."

"Now, now . . . ," said my pa. He dropped his voice and had a worried look on his face. "That ain't no way to talk in front of the young 'uns, here. You've got the wrong idea 'bout me."

Matthew turned to me and asked, "Is this man your father, Billy?"

"I reckon so," I answered. "I never seen him before, though."

"Oh yes, I'm his father. I even have somethin' to prove it. . . . Somethin' I've been carryin' around for twelve long years, just waitin' for this day."

He reached in his back pocket and pulled out a pile of folded up papers. "This here will end any type of argument about the situation."

Matthew took the paper and unfolded it.

"It's a baptism certificate for William Creekmore, Jr. . . . Well, that fixes it. This man's your father."

My dad slung his arm around my shoulder and pulled me to him. "I've got a lot to make up to you, Billy, and I'm gonna do it. I've waited a long time to have you by my side."

"So you're taking him with you, eh? Gonna have him join the Graftin Circus?" asked Matthew.

"Yes, sir, I am. A boy should be with his pa."

It was true, I thought, looking up in his face. I felt a pang of sadness when I realized I'd be leaving Rufus behind. I hoped he wouldn't be too upset about how things had turned out. We was building some plans together, but, out of nowhere, good fortune had come my way. I hoped he wouldn't begrudge me none.

"Good-bye, Billy," said Rufus. "Hope to run into you again someday." His freckled eyelids were blinking back tears.

"Now don't worry 'bout that," said my pa. "You'll be seeing each other again. The circus is like a big tribe broken up into little clans. We'll catch up with you sooner or later."

"So long, Rufus," I said. "Tell Darla I said so long, and thanks, Matthew, for bein' such a fair boss."

We waved good-bye, then turned in opposite directions along the tracks. Matthew and Rufus heading north, us heading south. A freight train was ambling outta the yard. Pa started running alongside it and threw his roll of posters inside the open door of one of the cars, then jumped aboard.

"Pick your feet up, Billy Creekmore!" he yelled. "C'mon, boy! Move it!"

For a moment I didn't know if I should turn tail and run, or jump aboard with him. I ain't never hopped a train, and that open door seemed awful high off the ground. My heart was pounding. The train was picking up speed and gaining some distance.

"C'mon, Billy!" My pa stuck out his hand for me. It was all I could see of him—his hand outstretched in the dark. How I knew what to do, I can't say, but I reached for him and ran along the train with all my might.

Somehow or other I made the leap, and my pa pulled me aboard the empty car.

"Yee-haw! You did it, Billy, hopped this train like a pro!" He slapped me on the back, laughing out loud. "Yessir, it's you and me now, boy. You and me!"

With all the excitement and noise, and the rocking of the train, I felt kinda sick to my stomach. I told my pa I thought I might throw up, but he said not to worry.

"If you do that's fine. Don't worry none about my clothes." He pulled me close, and in a little while, the bad feeling went away.

CHAPTER TWENTY-SIX

We Almost *Run into* SOME TROUBLE *with* THE LAW

I sat right on the floor of the car, just a coupla feet above the tracks, feeling every single bump and swerve. There warn't nothing inside to swallow up the noise, so it just banged around the car, echoing and thrashing till it filled up my whole head. I felt my bones shake, but it didn't bother my pa none. He was sleeping sound, dreaming away by the looks of it. His mouth was moving like he was deep in conversation.

As for me, I couldn't sleep a wink, and it wasn't just the noise and the rattling that stopped me, either. I was plain mystified at the sudden turn in my life. Not long ago, I was talking with Rufus about him being a clown and me being a trick rider with the Sparks Circus. Now I was on a freight train highballing into the night, my father sleeping beside me. It was what I had longed for when I was little, what Aunt Agnes had wished for me when she urged me to leave Holly Glen, but I had given up thinking it would ever happen. It's best not to get settled on things being a certain way, I realized. Life had a funny way of interrupting your plans.

I was thinking these things when the train began to slow down. The brakes screeched a long, long time, and eventually the train came to a halt. My pa jerked awake.

"Where are we?" I asked.

"Not sure. Did we pass a little town with a station on the main street?"

"Can't say," I answered. "If we did, it didn't have no lights."

"Hmm," Pa said. He stood up in the doorway and had himself a look around. Down the line some men were talking. Pa shushed me, then crouched down to listen. He turned to me a few moments later and whispered, "We're in a bit of trouble, Billy. This here's a rail yard filled with bulls."

"Bulls?"

"Railroad police. They're on patrol, looking for the likes of us—plain, poor folks that can't afford a ticket. They'll beat us up if they catch us, or take us to jail, or both."

My blood ran cold. Memories of the Baldwin-Felts guards and all their brutality flashed in my mind. "What'll we do?" I asked.

"We're gonna make a run for it. You've got to stick by me best as you can, and keep your mouth shut."

"Yes, sir," I whispered.

"You know how to Indian walk?"

"You mean walkin' on the outside of your feet?"

"That's right, son, and always heel to toe. Heel to toe on the outside of your feet. That's the quietest way to walk there is. Once we're off this train, we're gonna Indian walk to that clump of trees over yonder. You ready?"

"Yes, sir," I answered.

He picked up his roll of posters and tossed them to the ground, then, quiet as a cat, he jumped off the train. He grabbed me by the waist and helped me down. Before we took off, he nodded to the right for me to look. Not fifty feet away, two of the bulls was having themselves a smoke. The tips of their cigarettes glowed in the dark, and a shotgun was slung over the one's arm.

We crouched down as we headed into tall weeds along the tracks, Indian walking all the way until we reached the stand of locust trees. We barely made a rustle.

"Didn't I say you was a natural!" said my pa with delight. "I'm telling you, Billy, you've got talent to spare."

"Are we safe?" I asked.

"You bet. Bulls won't venture past the gravel. We'll spend the night here, then follow the tracks a few miles. We've got a ways to go before we catch up with the Graftin Circus."

Between the trees, the earth was soft and bare except for a blanket of leaves. It was good enough for a night's sleep, so we made our beds under the stars. Lightning bugs drifted by, and the night was filled with faint sounds. We didn't speak for a long time. Then I asked him the question I'd had for as long as I can remember.

"Pa, why didn't you come for me when I was at the orphanage?"

A tiny cloud of gnats buzzed overhead. It was a long time before he answered.

"Well, son . . . I didn't have much to give you. I didn't eat regular, didn't work regular, didn't have a home. Seemed to me that long as you was so little, Guardian Angels was the best place for you."

"It warn't," I said. "The Beadles kept us half starved, and Mr. Beadle beat us for no reason at all. Boys was hauled off to work in the glassworks and some of 'em died there."

"I always planned to come get you before you was of age for factory work. That was never gonna happen to you."

"But it almost did," I said, "'cause Mr. Beadle lied about our ages, and I was called up to go, but just in time, Uncle Jim came to get me. Then I went to live with him and Aunt Agnes in Holly Glen."

"You don't say . . . ," he said. His voice got a little tense, and I was afraid I had upset him. "How's Agnes? She still a healer?"

"Yes, sir," I said. I told him about the cave-in that killed Clyde and how Aunt Agnes bandaged the cuts and bones of the injured and helped the family of the dead in their grieving. Next thing you know, I told him about the UMW and the strike, and how the Baldwin-Felts agents came to break it up and killed Uncle Jim. My pa looked at the dark sky without sharing his thoughts.

"Aunt Agnes was the one who told me to find you. The Baldwin-Felts was comin' into town to round up those of us that broke away, so she grabbed some things for me and helped me off."

"Sounds like Agnes," he said. "She always was one to care for her family."

"You wrote her I was stillborn," I said. I felt nervous bringing it up. I didn't want him thinking I was ungrateful. He had just helped me escape the bulls and was taking me on as his own son, but the question nagged at me, and I had to ask. "Why'd you lie?"

"Billy, you ask hard questions. . . . Truth is, I was afraid Agnes might take you away from me. She disapproved of me, you know. Never said so to my face, but I could feel it," he said, pointing to his heart, "right here. I figured I'd tell her both you and your mother was dead, then I'd have the midwife take care of you till I got something steady. But it's been a broken path for me. The years ran together, and things didn't work out like I expected."

Pa looked away from me. He pulled out a little bottle from his hip pocket and took a long drink. I searched my mind for something cheery to say.

"And here we are, Pa! Together, just like we always wanted, just like you planned."

This seemed to take the sadness out of him. He looked back at me and smiled. "You're right, Billy! Here we are, together at last, off on an adventure!"

He talked easy now, telling me 'bout the carnivals and circuses he worked, taking another swig from his bottle every now and then. "I used to be 'circus simple,' which means a fella who loves the circus so much he don't want no other kinda life. Only that's no way to be at all, Billy, and you watch you don't get circus simple yourself. No, it's best to be free from all attachments in this world. Otherwise you make bad business decisions."

He told me the Graftin Circus was a low-class kinda circus, a regular fireball outfit, which was the name for a shoddy circus with second- and third-rate performers that had all sorts of dishonest things going on. Mr. Graftin didn't mind any of his crew working the crowds picking pockets as long as they gave him a percentage of the take.

"Oh, there's lots of tricks for taking folks' money, Billy. The ticket booth, for one. The Captain, for that's what Mr. Graftin likes to be called and don't you forget it, sets the booth about a foot higher than normal so folks can't see their change when it's laid down. He has the man at the booth hurry folks along so they don't even know they're shortchanged."

"That's terrible, Pa," I said. "It's stealin'."

"It's only pennies, Billy," he replied. "Anyone who notices gets his back, and those that don't count their change don't need it. It's just a little extra to feed the ponies."

It didn't seem right to me, but I let it rest. "Any trick riders in his show, Pa?"

"Used to be. Two Frenchmen, but they took off and joined another outfit."

Maybe my pa knew a thing or two 'bout trick riding, I thought.

It was a balmy night with milky stretches of stars. Every now and then a breeze lifted the leaves above us, and I should have been feeling drowsy and comfortable. But I wasn't. My mind was restless with vague thoughts and feelings. I tried sorting them out, but I couldn't. I gave up, figuring I was in shock. After all the postcards, the years of yearning and wondering, I knew I should be overjoyed. Instead, I felt sort of detached, like I was cut off and dangling in a different place. I didn't have words to describe how I felt about finally being with my pa. He was sound asleep beside me, and I listened to him breathe till I finally tired out.

CHAPTER TWENTY-SEVEN

We Meet Up with

THE GRAFTIN CIRCUS

and

I BECOME

A MIT READER

It was dawn when my pa woke me. He said we had to cover some miles before the heat of the day. We hiked a beaten path along the tracks. Pa got a move on, and I did my best to keep up while ignoring my hunger pangs. There'd be plenty of food once we caught up with the Captain, he said.

Sometime around noon, we passed a sorry looking little depot, then soon enough Pa found the Graftin

Circus camp. My heart kinda sank when I saw it. It warn't nothing more than a few dirty tents. The horses were tied up to a post with a bag of feed strapped to 'em. They was scrawny, angry looking beasts, twitching away flies. One was off to the side, sort of listless and weak looking. Pa said he had the shakes, which is a type of cold horses can get. Some folks were cooking over little campfires, while others were hanging up laundry or sitting on trunks playing cards. They was all men. There were no bally girls or lady acrobats, no fat ladies or lady tightrope walkers in sight.

"Didn't know you had a boy," said one old fella sitting on a bench. He wore a crumpled black hat and was chewing on a toothpick. He looked at me with sad eyes that wrinkled down at the corners. His name was Hank, and he was the manager of the sideshow.

"He's named Billy after me, and he's got a powerful way with words, just like his pa. You should hear the stories he's been tellin' me! Made me think he and I should work up an act—a mit reader show, only I'll be the shill and he'll be the palmist—the Boy Seer from the East! We could put him in a turban with a big old jewel at the front. We'll paint his face and line his eyes so he looks like he's from India."

Pa had it all worked out. I'd be sitting in a booth inside the sideshow with rows of benches lined up in front of me. One of the fellas from the band would play some Eastern type music, and once the benches filled, Pa'd be my first customer.

"I could ask him if I should open up a hardware store, or whether I'll get over the gout or not, or if my uncle was gonna leave me any money. Now, Billy, here's where you get to use all your acting and storytelling talent. You gotta look at my palms for a while, then close your eyes and open your mouth a little, like you was receiving word from beyond. Then you speak in an accent and tell my fortune, only make sure it's always a good fortune 'cause folks won't pay to hear bad news. Oh, Hank, it'll be a wonderful show. Folks'll love it, being how he's just a boy. . . ."

Hank chewed away at his toothpick and listened. His eyes looked sad as ever, but he said it was a fine idea, just might bring in a good purse.

" 'Course," said he, "we'll need a new poster with his

picture on it. Got to get Norm working on that. . . ."

"Oh, sure, Norm'll do a great job. If the paint dries in time, we'll have the act ready for the next town."

Hank nodded and said okay, and go take a look through the costume trunk for that turban, then let Norm get a good look at me so he could get started on the poster, and so on and so forth.

Well, we found the turban and a glass jewel to pin on the front. Pa went off to have a chat with some fellas, and while I was sitting still for Norm to sketch me, along come old man Graftin, only I remembered to call him Captain like Pa said I should.

"And who are you?" he said. He was long and skinny, in a wrinkled black suit with tails and a tattered top hat. He had a beard along his chin like President Lincoln, only it was scraggly and white. He gave the appearance of an old man, only he walked quick and upright.

"I'm Billy Creekmore, Captain," I said.

"Young Billy Creekmore. Billy Creekmore the Second—for are you or are you not the son of that brilliant, daring grifter William Creekmore?"

He had the fanciest way of talking of anyone I'd ever heard. His voice trilled here and there, especially about the *r* and *l* sounds, just like he was on stage reciting Shakespeare. His manners were so fine, they made me forget some of my hesitation 'bout reading and telling fortunes.

"Yes, sir, I am."

"A marvelous man! I've had the pleasure of knowing him these past three years. He's made me many, many dollars, and for that I am exceedingly grateful. . . . Now, I understand you and your father are putting together a fortunetelling act. The Boy Seer from the East! Or something to that effect . . ."

"That's right, sir. The costume's all figured out and Norm's already workin' on the poster."

"I am very pleased, very pleased. My advice, young Billy, is to work on your accent! Adjust your mannerisms! Become that young seer from the East! Feel it! Live it! If you do it right, you'll be taking the suckers right and left!"

Later that night, while he was cooking us some potatoes over a little fire, I told my pa about meeting the

Captain, and how I didn't want to cheat anyone out of his money.

"Now, now don't let the Captain bother you. He's awful singleminded about money. Makes him miss the finer points of things. Telling fortunes ain't like what he says at all." He went on, "You won't be cheating folks, Billy, you'll be helping by telling 'em things they want to hear."

"How is that gonna help 'em?"

"You see, Billy, the world's full of sadness and loss. You know that from your own life now, don't you? When folks come to see you, they're sick with suffering. Telling 'em things is gonna work out eases their minds. It's like passing out medicine."

I turned it over in my mind. It sounded right enough. What good was telling someone desperate or hopeful, that, no, the fates warn't looking kindly on him? Why not pretend to know the future and tell folks that everything was gonna be rosy? It couldn't do no harm. In fact, it might just do 'em a world of good.

The Graftin Circus was laid up for a few more days on account of that one sick pony, just long enough for the poster to dry. The painting showed me dressed in a spangled shirt with droopy sleeves wearing the jeweled turban. My eyes was half closed and I had a kinda wise and peaceful look on my face. The background was dark purple with swirly gold stars and fiery comets here and there. Pa and I practiced our act, working out the details. He had me work on the way I used my hands when I spoke, pointing up to the sky every now and then and making my hands kinda delicate like I'd never done a day of hard labor in my life, only meditating and reading fortunes, and talking to spirits from the Great Beyond.

Pa was certain we'd be a great success. He got near wild with joy thinking up variations to our act. Depending on the crowd, he'd play his role joyful or hearty. If half the crowd was men, he'd pretend to be a businessman asking for advice about where he should set his store or what sort of thing he should import from China. If there was mostly women, he'd pretend to be the sweetheart of a girl whose parents were against him. He coached me hard, teaching me to talk in an accent and telling me to be sure to paint my arms past my elbows. There was a lot to keep in my mind, and, on top of that, I had to be ready to think on my feet. This warn't ever a problem for me in the past, but I warn't sure I could do it in front of a paying audience.

Once the troupers nursed that horse back to health, we was hopscotching from one place to the next, doing our best to land in town the day before one of the bigger, glitzier outfits so we could steal their audience. Every advance crew at the Sparks Circus had been approved by the mayor or the sheriff long before it ever pulled in, but the Captain never bothered to ask permission to bring the Graftin Circus to town. Pa said only the rich shows could afford to do things on the up and up and still put on a quality show. The rest had to cut corners where they could.

Somewhere in Missouri I put on my first show. The other sideshow acts and I were in our places. I could hear Old Hank outside the tent, barking at folks through his megaphone about the Mysterious House of Mirrors, Rolando the Snake Man of the Amazon, who was actually one of the roustabouts painted up to look like he had scales, and me, the Boy Seer from the East, fortune-teller to the Crowned Heads of Europe. I was, he said, due to return to the palace of the Raj and this would be my last performance in the States. By my side, dressed in harem pants and wearing a fez, was Mitch, one of the musicians, playing some slinky music on his clarinet. I was painted and costumed, sitting at a little round table before a crystal ball. Above me a chandelier of burning candles cast flickering shadows. Folks drifted in after seeing Rolando and getting lost in the maze. Once the benches were filled, Mitch introduced me to the crowd.

"Ladies and gentlemen, boys and girls, behold Hadji, the Boy Seer from the East. Descended from a long line of sorcerers and clairvoyants, Hadji sees both the future and the past, both this world and the next. Would anyone here care to ask a question of the Boy Seer for the price of a nickel?"

My pa, dressed in a Sunday suit and sitting toward the back, shot up his hand.

"If only you could tell me," he called out, "is my sweet wife finally at peace after her long illness? Does she miss me, her true love, and the darling life we shared together?"

The question startled me. We hadn't rehearsed this one. My own sadness about missing my mother came over me, and I nearly broke into tears. Why did he do this? I wondered. Was he trying to trick me into a good performance? Someone started to cough. A baby cried. The audience was growing restless, waiting for an answer. I tilted my head back, closed my eyes, and opened my palms to the audience.

"Your wife sends you her deepest love . . ." I took a deep breath before going on. "She wants you to know that her days with you in the little white cottage by the lake . . . were her happiest ever . . . on this earth. But do not worry for her, she says, for her pain is gone."

"Oh, lordy, lordy, lordy!" My pa could wail up a storm when he wanted. "Oh, I can see that cottage and remember those days like they was yesterday! What else does she say? What else?"

"She wants you to know . . . that she is at peace . . . dwellin' in Heaven among the angels, playin' a harp, stoppin' her music only . . . to look down from Heaven at you. . . ."

Every woman in the crowd broke into tears. Even

the men got sentimental, blowing their noses and shuffling in their seats. My pa put a nickel in Mitch's hand, saying thank you, thank you, and up shot a host of hands waving for attention. Mitch had to ask folks to please be patient, saying that everyone who wanted would get a chance to ask me a question. Old ladies wanted to know how their dead husbands was getting on, young men wanted to know if they should go prospecting in Alaska, and pretty young ladies asked me if their sweethearts was true. With all those yearning faces staring at me, my storytelling abilities took off. I didn't have no problem at all coming up with forecasts and predictions for my customers. At first I felt uneasy, but soon enough it was just like the old days at the orphanage, when my tales could make the boys stop in their tracks and all eyes were on me. Truth be told, it was a powerful feeling, and I liked it.

The act brought in quite a purse, which pleased the Captain considerable. He slapped us on our backs, slipped us a few coins, and gave my pa a bottle of whisky. In fact, the act worked so well that the Captain took me off the work crew and told me not to change my costume or take off my makeup till the last customer left the grounds. Some of the troupers got jealous since I didn't help strike the tent or groom the horses like everyone else. They called me fancy pants and said I was highfaluting and full a frills, asking me who did I think I was not to be down in the dirt working with the rest of 'em. Once Mr. Graftin overheard, and he marched over in his topcoat and hat, his coattails whipping about his legs.

"This boy's bringing me a passel of money, and I don't want anyone recognizing him. All it'd take is one smart aleck to recognize him pulling out a stake with his makeup off and it'd blow the gaff. Word spreads, boys, word spreads."

And that was that. I didn't get no more teasing or threats since folks was scared of the Captain, even though he was just a skinny old man. But I knew my days as the Boy Seer wouldn't last. One night I heard the Captain arguing with one of the roustabouts, an angry guy who was used mostly for his muscle since he had no gift for con games or performing of any kind. He was angry and drunk, saying he was sick and tired of me lolling about while he was working like heck to keep up with the pace of the show, and it seemed like he was gonna heel it outta the show or else slug the Captain or anyone else he could get his hands on.

"Ah, now, Mike," crooned the Captain as he passed him a flask, "it's a short run. He can't be the Boy Seer forever."

CHAPTER TWENTY-EIGHT

Despairing Over a Question, I'm Forced TO TAKE A STAND

Summer crept into fall, and the Graftin Circus kept moving on. There were good towns and bad towns, towns that turned out in full to see the show and towns that seemed to know it warn't quality entertainment and gave us the cold shoulder. All in all, I was losing enthusiasm for being the Boy Seer from the East. I could just imagine Clayton shaking his head with disgust at the whole shenanigans.

"What's the matter with you, Billy?" Pa had a pointed look on his face. He was straightening the lapels of his suit, ready to take on his role as a bereaved widower asking the Boy Seer the first question of the night. "You seem distracted."

"I guess I am," I said. I was dabbing makeup on my arms and face. Early that morning, we pulled into a grim little town somewhere in southern Illinois. The roads was unpaved and the sidewalks was nothing more than broken railroad ties covered with dirt. All the buildings was sad-faced and dusty.

"Folks'll be coming to see you, Billy. They'll be wanting answers to their questions, a word or two from their dearly departed. Don't you want to help the folks forget their miseries?"

"Yes," I said.

"Then what's wrong with you?"

"I guess I didn't sleep much," I replied. "Got a crick in my neck."

"Well, get it uncricked," he said. Then he opened the tent flap and left. For a second, just before the flap closed, I caught a glimpse of folks' shoes. There was worn boots and scuffed heels, and a set of dirty bare feet running along. Kid's feet. Probably a boy, I figured, though I couldn't tell for sure. I hoped he didn't step on a nail or a piece of glass, for Heaven knows there was plenty about.

I was surprised so many folks in such a sad little town showed up for the circus. Every seat in the sideshow was filled, and folks were standing on tippy toes at the back, applauding when I made my entrance. 'Bout a dozen hands shot up when Mitch asked if there was anyone who'd like to ask the Boy Seer from the East a question.

"You, sir!" Mitch said, calling on my father. "You may ask Hadji the first question of the night."

"Thank you, thank you," dithered my pa, histrionic as ever. "I've come to ask about my dearly departed wife, the sweetest creature that ever graced God's green earth . . ."

As if he was overcome with emotion, Pa dropped his head in his hands, and I noticed something laced through his fingers, sparkling in the candlelight. Of course, he knew I'd catch anything new in the act quick as a snap. A second later, he looked at me and held up my mother's necklace.

"This necklace . . . ," he whimpered, ". . . is the only thing I have left from my dear, sweet wife. Tell me, Boy Seer from the East, is she resting peacefully?"

I don't know if I was angry or shocked, but I couldn't catch my breath at first. He must have snuck back to our tent after I had left for the sideshow to rifle through my tin box and take my mother's necklace. How could he use the only thing I had of my mother's like this? The thought of it made me sick, and it was all I could do to go on with the show.

Somehow, though, I managed, and Pa and I completed our routine. The audience went wild with grief. Hankies fluttered left and right as ladies sniffled and cried. There were the usual widows and widowers asking for news from the beyond, and sweethearts asking if their lover was true. I watched and listened, trying to figure out what they wanted most to hear, then gave it back to them in an accented voice with half-closed eyes. I was going by rote, still angry at my pa, but well trained enough so that I could do my job. I didn't take no joy in it that night. It was a sad house, and there were more than the usual amount of troubling questions. When an old lady asked about her missing son, and a boy not much older than me asked about his sick baby sister, I felt downright bleak.

Pa, on the other hand, was happy as could be. He couldn't understand why I was sad about the folks and their troubles or upset about my mother's necklace.

"I don't ever want to use it in a show, Pa. It ain't right. It's disrespectful to her memory."

"Didn't know you had any memory of her, Billy."

"And I don't want you touchin' it again! Keep your hands off my things!"

"C'mon now, Billy, don't be mad at me." He smiled. "I had to get you in the right mood. You were gonna blow the act. I knew your mother's necklace would wake you up! Hey, cheer up now and forgive your old pa. We made over ten dollars tonight. It's just like I always say—the sadder the town, the better the money."

At the end of the night, Pa nearly danced over to the Captain to give him his half. The Captain was so pleased, he gave Pa a bottle of whisky, and the two of them sat up drinking with Hank.

Alone in my tent, feeling dreary, I pulled out my old datebook from the Sparks Circus just to see where they was. It warn't more than a few months since Rufus, Matthew, and I were printing up posters and pasting up a town, but it seemed a lifetime ago. The three of us was a good team. Most days we finished just in time to make it back to camp by supper. The waiters served us potatoes and steak, soup or stew, cake or pie, take what you please. Mr. Sparks and his wife always ate with us, and they always stopped to ask us about the towns ahead, and if we thought we'd play to a full house.

I got awful lonely going over these memories. Once I was a union man, then I was a member of the Sparks World Famous Circus. Now I was part of a small-time circus working the graft. I wondered if everything folks said about me back at the orphanage was true—that I was born to be unlucky, that I'd always have to fight the Devil inside me, that I was prone to taking a bad path through life filled with deception and lies. All the feelings I used to have of spirits yearning to talk to me were gone. My heart was growing cold from the folks I was living with and the lies I was telling. It was just like Peggy told me so long ago.

Our run was near over, and we had only a few more towns to visit before we went to North Carolina. The Captain had some land near Charlotte that he used for our winter quarters, but Pa said it warn't gonna be any kinda vacation. That was the time we'd be repairing the wagons, patching the tents, touching up the paint, and getting ready for the next tour. My birthday and Christmas warn't that far away, and I kinda hoped we might celebrate them somehow. It would be our first ones together as father and son. Maybe we could go into Charlotte and see the lights and the window displays, I suggested, but Pa said there wouldn't be no time for that.

"Too much work to do," he said, "and we won't be making any money. Sorry, boy. Ain't gonna be no birthday or Christmas presents."

"That's okay, Pa. Presents don't matter none," I said.

It was the end of a long, drizzly day. Only a few folks had ventured out in the gloom to see the circus, and only a few of them paid the extra money to see the sideshow. Once inside, only three folks asked me questions. Pa was tired. We was heating some beans over a smoky campfire. He took a swig from his flask and wiped his mouth with the back of his hand.

"Once we're in North Carolina, you'll be working like the rest of us, Billy. No need for you to act the part of the Boy Seer night and day. You'll be learning a whole new set of skills. Like how to shoe a horse and guy out the tent ropes."

I said I'd be happy to learn, but Pa said it warn't gonna be any fun. "These smaller outfits are too much work, Billy. I work twice as hard for the Captain as I did for Mr. John Robinson and his Sunday school show. Somehow or other, we've got to get ourselves outta here, Billy. We could take our act anywhere! Maybe we should steal your poster and one of the ponies and fly outta here right now."

"No, Pa, we can't do that," I said. "It's not right."

"What'd you say to me, boy?" He turned on me with a vengeful look. "Are you defying me? Do you think you know better than me? What makes you think you know what's right?"

He had never said anything like this to me before, and I was scared he might hit me.

"Think you're better than your old man, don't you? Got yourself a prize booth in the sideshow, don't you? Well, who do you think got you started? It was me!"

He kicked the pot of beans off the fire. Some of 'em splashed my way and burned my legs. "You ain't better than me, Billy. You ain't nothing but a nitpicking lackey, just another gunsel working for the Captain, doing what he tells ya, not thinking for yourself. . . ."

He threw his empty flask at my feet. "Go find Hank," he said. "Tell him to fill my bottle or else I'll come looking for him."

I scampered off looking for Hank or anyone else who'd spare some whisky. A few of the men were drinking round a fire outside Hank's tent.

"It ain't whisky." Mitch laughed. "But your pa won't notice. Not in the state he's in."

This set the circle into sloppy, open-mouthed laughter. One of 'em fell over, he was laughing so hard. I remembered the miners crumpled with drink on payday, and how Uncle Jim said drink can ruin a man. How far was my pa from being ruined? I wondered as Mitch filled his flask, then I hurried back to our tent, hoping he wouldn't be mad at me for taking too long.

When I got back, my pa was sitting by the fire. He looked up at me with bleary eyes. "I'm sorry I yelled at you, son. Forget what I said and forgive your old man." He dropped his head in his hands and cried a little. "I yelled at your mother sometimes, but she didn't hold it against me, so you can't either. Oh, Billy, we coulda had a different life, like that white cottage by the lake in our act. If only your mother hadn't died . . ."

"Don't, Pa," I said. "Be quiet now. I don't hold nothin' against you." He quieted down enough to take a few sips outta the bottle I brought him. Then he seemed to pass out. I was glad. I didn't want him to talk no more.

Days later we was somewhere in Kentucky, setting up our tents in a coal town. The little houses were tackety and run down, just like the patch villages in West Virginia, Holly Glen included. Some of 'em had paper instead of glass over the window frames, and most of the trees was scrawny and twisted, stunted and choking from years of coal dust. It was morning, and I was checking the ropes of the sideshow tent, making sure they was taut, and moving the stakes out some if they warn't. Hank and my pa were off unfolding the canvas of the big tent, and I was alone for the moment when two little kids, a boy and a girl, came up to me. They was brother and sister, I guessed, and the boy's fingertips and nose were solid black. He was younger than me and already working the mines.

"You the fortune-telling boy?" the girl asked. She was the younger one, no more than seven years old, but not shy like her brother. Her brother seemed to be about nine but was sort of distracted, looking off here and there, not saying anything.

"I reckon so," I said.

"You're a lot paler than your poster," she said.

"Ah, they just paint it that way so folks'll think I'm from India."

"But you ain't," she said. She wasn't angry 'bout the fib, just setting things straight in her mind.

"No, I ain't."

"Well, can you tell fortunes? Like the poster says?" She was little and bold, awful cute in the way a few wispy strands of her hair fell about her face.

"Why don't your brother do the talkin'? He's the older one."

"He don't like talkin' no more. So, can you tell fortunes or not?"

"Just wait here a moment. I'll get things ready."

I slipped inside the tent, found my turban, and lit the candles, all the while thinking that they seemed like nice kids who wouldn't mind that I wasn't painted up or had the music going like in the regular show. I decided not to ask 'em for money since they didn't look like they had none, and after all no one ever did in a coal camp. Truth be told, I didn't like pulling into these towns, knowing what I did about life in the mines and how the company rigged things against the miners and their families something fierce.

I ushered the kids in, saying I'd tell their fortunes for free, and that afterward they could walk through the House of Mirrors if they wanted.

"Some circuses call it the Crystal Maze, but we say it's the House of Mirrors. It's all the same. . . . You wander about lookin' at different types of fun mirrors, some that make you squat, some that make you wavy or skinny. You go along lookin' at yourselves in different ways, gettin' lost in the maze till finally you find your way out."

"Do folks always find their way out?" the girl asked.

"Most times," I said. "But you won't get lost for long, I can tell."

Well, the little girl took the seat at the table while her brother stood behind her, holding his cap with his black fingers and looking for all the world like a lost soul. The more I looked at him the more he reminded me of Herbert Mullens, the boy Mr. Beadle beat so bad he stopped talking.

"What's your question?"

"What I wanna know . . . ," she began, only her voice started to catch and she had to stop before going on, 'cause the tears started coming out heavy. "What I wanna know is if our pa's gonna get better. There was a cave-in, and he's in the hospital with a crushed leg. The doctor says he ain't gonna walk again, but I'm hoping you can tell us something different."

I'd been asked plenty of questions like this before,

but not in a coal camp, and not by a child. It warn't easy to give her my usual reply, which was, oh yes, he'll pull through just fine, say your prayers and have faith.

But that's exactly what I did say. I looked at her palm a bit, then closed my eyes and tilted back my head, acting for all the world like I was communicating with spirits, which as I said I couldn't do no more. I could feel all the worry in the little girl's heart, and how almost all the feelings in her brother was nearly shut up forever because of the harshness of the mine. Maybe he'd grow up to be a ruined man like my pa, or else he might die young like Clyde Light.

I was feeling those things, the girl's love for her pa, the boy's silence, and then, for the first time in a long, long time, I felt a spirit come to me. It was a woman's spirit, a mother, I reckoned, maybe my own. I couldn't tell, but I felt it hovering above us, embracing us in a way, and my heart seemed to grow in both sadness and love. She didn't have no words, but she guided me to say what I did.

"Your pa's gonna get better real soon, but your life's gonna change some in a way I can't predict. Keep a candle lit and say some prayers at your church whenever you can. But don't worry none, cause there's a flock of angels lookin' over your family."

Well, the little girl and her brother just about lit up hearing this, and she thanked me over and over, saying I was a right good fortune-teller and what exactly did Heaven look like, and did the angels have wings of feathers or were they made of stardust, and so on and so forth. My words came easy enough, but the spirit was already leaving us. I told her Heaven looked like it was made of cotton candy, and the angels' wings was either silver or gold, but I was getting awful uneasy talking to 'em. My nerves was shook up, and I started feeling kinda panicky like I might cry. So, I pretended something had come to my mind all of a sudden, and I took 'em to the House of Mirrors.

"Why don't you come with us?" she asked. "C'mon, it'll be fun. We can chase each other."

"Oh no, I got things to do. Besides I been there too many times and it ain't no fun for me no more."

And so I left 'em in the maze. They was in high spirits 'cause of the good news I gave 'em, and I could even hear the brother laughing as I left the sideshow tent and walked out to find my pa.

I couldn't do this no more. I was leaving, simple as that. I threw my turban to the ground and kicked it away. Back at my tent, I rustled through a pile of clothes till I found my tin box. I tore up every single card my pa ever sent me. I slipped my mother's broken necklace into my pocket, then I left.

"I see you've been starting your show early," said my pa when he saw me stomping cross the grounds. "How much did you take those kids for?"

"I didn't take 'em for nothin'. I told 'em a fortune for free, then I let 'em go in the maze, and I'd give 'em some cotton candy if it was made, and a pet chameleon, or a whistle if I knew where the Captain kept 'em."

"Why the heck did you do that? You're talking foolish, boy. What's got into you?" he asked. He shielded his eyes from the sun, wincing a bit. I could tell he was achy and hungover from the night before. He didn't really want an answer to his question, but I felt like giving him one anyway.

"I'm tired of cheatin' folks outta their money and

pretendin' to be something I'm not." My eyes were stinging with tears and I felt dumb and stupid, like any kid does when he starts to cry in front of folks and can't stop. "I hate you and I hate the Captain. I'm leavin', goin' off by myself, 'cause I can't do this no more. I can't go on takin' 'vantage of folks that's poor and downhearted 'cause their father's near dyin' or they've been broken down by the mines. Why, you and the Captain's as bad as Mr. Newgate and the coal barons, and Mr. Colder at the glass factory."

"I don't know what you're talking 'bout, but you ain't going anywhere."

"I am, too," I said, and I started to run off, only he lurched at me and grabbed the back of my collar. "Let me go!" I screamed, trying to squirm away.

"C'mon, now, Billy. Settle down. I'll take you into town and buy you an ice cream," he said. "Let's sit down and talk about our plans."

"I don't want any plans with you!" I yelled. "I never did." I twisted fierce enough to break his grip, then I darted off. He stumbled after me and fell.

"All right then, Billy," he yelled. "If you wanna go, go.

Although I think you're leaving a swell setup, Boy Seer from the East."

And those was the last words he said, and he didn't even call me by my real name, only the name he made up for me, which made me think he didn't really know me or love me after all, even though he was my own flesh and blood.

CHAPTER TWENTY-NINE

I Head SOUTH, *Trying to Find* MY WAY HOME

I ran outta camp without looking back, running like I did from the guards when they shot Uncle Jim and Clayton. I knew enough about coal camps to find my way out.

Days passed, and I was back to my old ways, alone in the woods, my clothes ragged, my bones beginning to show 'cause the only food I had was the berries I picked and the vegetables I stole from a farm I passed by. Every now and then, when I was really hungry, I'd knock on a door asking folks if I could paint a fence or milk a cow for whatever food they could spare.

Strangely, I warn't at all sad or downhearted. And I warn't lonely, either, for the spirits were back with me. They were nature spirits, spirits of the earth that felt kindly toward humans, and they hung close to the old paths I followed through the woods. Every now and then, when I had a drink from a stream or rested under a willow, I felt them helping me along. I was altogether more hopeful than I ever was during any of my wanderings in the past. For the first time in my life, I knew where I was going.

"Where you off to?" asked an old woman. She lived in a little house near the tracks, and I had knocked on her door asking if I could do some chores in exchange for a meal. Her eyes were soft and kind behind her spectacles, and she sat with me on her porch while I ate the cold chicken she gave me.

"I'm headin' back to the Sparks Circus," I said. I pulled out the datebook from my back pocket to show her. "I used to work the advance crew for Mr. Sparks, all before a few bad things happened to me. If they're runnin' to schedule, which they usually do, they'll be pullin' into Charleston, South Carolina, right about now. They spend the winter just outside the city."

"Oh, the Sparks Circus is a fine show! They came through here 'bout five years ago and folks still talk about it."

"Yes, ma'am, I bet they do. Mr. Sparks puts on a quality show, no doubt about it."

"So you're heading down south to meet up with him. Going back to work the advance."

"Yes, ma'am, till I finish up my year of obligation, then I got plans. I'm gonna be a trick rider. Gonna train with the Christiani family. They're world famous, you know. See, if we want, Mr. Sparks lets us train as performers after we work the advance for a year. He'd let me be a clown or a trapeze flyer if I wanted, but I've got my heart set on bein' a trick rider."

"Do you now?"

"Yes, ma'am," I said. I cleaned out the old lady's gutters, then I clipped some branches that was brushing against her windows. I didn't want to take the two silver dollars she gave me—the meal was payment enough for my work—but she insisted. I slipped the coins in my pocket next to my mother's necklace.

"There's a train that runs all the way from here to Charleston," she said. "Use the money to buy a ticket. I'll be praying for you, Billy," she said, waving me good-bye.

"Thank you, ma'am," I called back.

I thought about hopping the train so I could save the money the old woman gave me, but it didn't seem like the right thing to do. I paid for my ticket and settled in for a long ride. I was the dirtiest one on board and more than a little embarrassed by my general appearance. I tipped my cap over my face, nestled into the window, and fell asleep.

The train rumbled along deep in Appalachia, stopping at one little mountain town after another. A day later, the mountains smoothed into soft hills and the terrain started to flatten out. We was getting closer and closer to the coast.

"Next stop, ladies and gentlemen—Charles-ton, South Car-o-lin-a," sang the conductor.

"Tell me, sir," I asked him before he sailed off to the

next car, "do you know where Mr. Charlie Sparks and his circus makes camp?"

"You fixin' to join the circus, boy?" he asked me. He had a craggy old face with bushy eyebrows.

"I already belong, sir," I said. "I got lost."

"Stay on this train one more stop," he said. "When you get off, head east about a mile and you'll find his camp. Got a nice set of cabins for his folks. Regular little town. You can't miss it."

He went on to say we'd be in the station for a coupla hours, and that I might like to take a little walk around the city.

"Charleston's one of the prettiest little cities you ever could see," he said.

"Thank you, sir," I said, "but I'm gonna stay right here." I couldn't possibly risk not getting back in time.

"Suit yourself," he said.

Those two hours took forever. I walked through the cars from one end to the other, trying to kill time. A few folks were left on the train, sleeping or reading, crocheting or writing a letter. I looked at their luggage on the racks and tried to figure out where they was going, but mostly I kept thinking about meeting up with the Sparks Circus. I hoped I'd find the camp all right and hoped I wasn't gonna be too early. I checked the route map again and figured they should be there by now, but you never knew for sure. Maybe they hit some bad weather along the way.

Porters loaded with luggage, families, old ladies with their companions, businessmen, and workers began boarding the train, and I figured it was near time to leave. I got back to my seat, and the engine started puffing and before long we rolled outta the station, my eyes glued to the window. It warn't more than a half-hour ride to the next stop. I jumped to the platform, figured where the sun rose, then took off.

It must have rained a day or so ago, for the edges of the dirt road was hard with dried mud. I could see the impressions of horseshoes, wagon wheels, and boots. *They're here!* I thought, my heart soaring. I broke into a run, and sure enough I came upon a sweet little collection of cabins. Each one had a chimney with a curlicue of smoke. One of 'em had pink gingham curtains hanging in the window, and, sure enough, there was Darla waddling down the steps, shooing away an old dog.

"Darla!" I cried, waving my hat at her.

"Billy Creekmore?" she yelled back, peering at me. "Is that you?"

"Yes," I cried. I ran into her soft arms and she kissed me on the top of my head.

"It's 'bout time you came back," she said.

"I know," I answered.

I'd be lying if I said I wasn't holding back a few tears. Finally, I was home, back with people who loved me and wanted me to be who I was. Pretty soon I'd be shaking hands with my old friends, and then Rufus and I would be off scouting around camp and catching up with each other. I could see myself, clear as day, riding bareback on a stallion. Oh, it'd be something to see, something Uncle Jim would stand up for. The stallion's mane would be ripplin' and I'd learn to stand up on his back, my arms outstretched. I'd be feeling all those spirits that follow me. They'd be riding with me, while the stallion galloped and the crowd cheered us on.

AUTHOR'S NOTE

When I first started thinking about the book that would become *Billy Creekmore,* I thought about the books that meant a great deal to me, books that concerned children alone in the world, working for their living and scrambling to simply grow up. It didn't take me long to realize that the books I loved most, both then and now, were those by Charles Dickens and Mark Twain. *Oliver Twist, Huckleberry Finn, David Copperfield,* and *Great Expectations,* among others, all deal with children who were ill treated or abandoned by parents and society. I loved following the rise and fall of the main character's fortunes, how each chapter began with its own suspenseful title and ended with a sentence that made you want to turn the page. These books—suspenseful, traditionally structured, plot and character bound—became my model for *Billy Creekmore.*

I began to research child labor in the United States and incorporate elements from my family history into a narrative. I was fortunate to have a landscape that called to me and became the setting for my book. My father was born and raised in a small Appalachian town on the Ohio River. I remember the long drive from our home in Columbus to Ironton, Ohio, and how I used to look out the car window at the small towns along the way. The smell of minerals was in the air, and the broken edges of the hills around my grandmother's house were veined with coal. From her house, it was only a short drive to the coal camps and hollers where children like Billy lived. I was in grade school then, reading *Tom Sawyer* and *The Secret Garden,* and listening to my father's stories of growing up on the river and roaming the woods.

Like Billy, my mother, Susan Morcone, spent time in a foster home at a working farm. She, too, was abandoned by her father after her mother died in childbirth, and was later adopted by her aunt and uncle. To this day, she is afraid of cows, goats, chickens, and mules. Because of her stories about being chased by geese and nipped by a pony, the typical peaceful farm scene has always read false to me. On my father's side, my great-grandfather and his mother were sent to debtor's prison after his father drowned off the coast of Liverpool.

Eventually, my great-grandfather was indentured to help pay off the family debt to a farmer in northern England. He was badly beaten and near starved, so this adventurous relative of mine stowed away on a boat to Canada (an illegal immigrant!), where he found his way to a kind baker who taught him the trade. Much of my immigrant family experienced the harsh face of late nineteenth- and early twentieth-century capitalism.

I spent five years researching and writing *Billy Creekmore*. I read everything I could find about the early years of coal mining in West Virginia, the daily lives and struggles of the boys working the mines, the United Mine Workers and the battle to unionize the coal industry, and how and why joining the circus would seem to be a terrific alternative to life in the mines. On a ten-day road trip with my father and my brother James, we drove through southern Ohio and West Virginia, exploring coal towns, hollers, and bends in the river. We walked through Matewan, West Virginia, and saw where the bullets from a gun battle between striking miners and Baldwin-Felts agents are still lodged in a brick building on the main street in town. We visited the Beckley Exhibition Coal Mine and spent an hour deep in the mine (more than enough time, I can assure you. It's spooky down there!). The next afternoon, in the archives of the West Virginia State Museum in Charleston, I had the great opportunity to look through a very old book that recorded the deaths of miners in the early years of the twentieth century. I found the names of many boys who were killed in the mines, and recorded them in the notebook I devoted to taking notes and scribbling ideas for my book. I wasn't sure why I wrote down so many names at the time, but I found them haunting and beautiful, names such as Clyde Light, Frank Moon, Rufus Twilly, and Golden Breedlove. Eventually I realized that one part of my book wanted to be a memorial of sorts to these boys, so, with the exception of the title character, every boy character in *Billy Creekmore* is named after a boy who died in a mining accident before reaching his seventeenth birthday.

I also traveled to Sarasota, Florida, to spend some time with my stepfather, Larry Short, and his wife, Roberta. They had long told me about the Ringling Circus Museum, and thanks to them my knowledge of the early American circus deepened considerably. The curators at the museum were kind enough to let me look through their archives, and many of the facts and details of Billy's experiences with the Sparks and Graftin circuses are based on what I uncovered there. Charles Sparks, the great, benevolent circus owner, is a historical person, and I was thrilled to look through one of the few remaining copies of the Sparks Circus route book, just like the one Billy looks at when he's feeling lonesome for his old friends. Captain Graftin is not a historical person, but his character is an amalgam of several of the grifters and showmen I read about.

It's often said that everyone's story is unique, but I'm more interested in how our stories are similar. All of us are haunted by scraps of memory, family history, books we've read, and stories we've been told. These elements are elusive and powerful, like the spirits that visit Billy. Should we choose to listen, they'll connect us like an invisible web, holding past and present, the distant and familiar together. I hope Billy's story encourages my readers to connect to children like him, to other books, and to their own family stories.